W0028238

Original Cover Art by Heather Fisher

heather-fisher.com

By the same Author

Themis Series Book: One We Were Swans

Themis Series Book Two: Tell Me There's a Reason

Available on Amazon

Table of Contents

But in a solitary life, there are rare moments when another soul dips near yours, as stars once a year brush the earth. Such a constellation was he to me.

Madeline Miller

PAUL

This was bad. The train ticket they'd given him was taking him to somewhere he'd never been before, to deliver a package to someone he didn't know, and no matter how many times he'd done this, Paul was shitting himself.

His seat was comfortable enough, but Paul wasn't. Subdued, troubled, he cuddled the weight of the rucksack on his lap like a sinister baby, and stared without seeing, a bystander not a witness, out into the countryside clattering by. He'd left his city behind hours ago and was hungry.

Breakfast had been a silent, brooding affair, wordlessly expressed distrust eyeing him across the table, a cereal bowl clattered carelessly in front of him where before a gentle slide and a smile had been the norm. He'd had to fetch his spoon himself. The body language of his parents said it all. *We may have to feed you, but we don't have to feel happy about it.*

Paul couldn't remember the last time he'd felt anything other than shame or fear and neither emotion could be avoided. He had to go home, he wanted to go to school, or at least, he used to. There was no escape. All he could do was keep going. Keep hoping that one day, his nightmare would be over, that he could tell them what was happening to him. Could explain why their son had turned from studious, willing, and polite schoolboy to a sullen, wordless truant.

He hoped that in the future no-one would ever know, that he would somehow manage to escape the consequences of today and a hundred others. That this would stop, he'd be released, his life would return to normal, and no explanations would be needed. That they'd put the current 'him' down to the unwelcome but necessary transition from childhood to adolescence and that years from now, perhaps on his graduation from Uni, or even his wedding day, they'd all be smiling again, the way it used to be.

That first day in the classroom, when this had all started, it had been ok at first. Tyrone, one of the cool kids, had startled him by taking the habitually empty workstation next to his and cosied up. *Mate, I need some help. You're good at this stuff, right?* Paul had twitched, at once wary, *Mate?* life experience warning him that to the guaranteed loud amusement of the rest of the class, this was more likely a prelude to a put down or a smack than a friendly overture. But Tyrone had persisted, had quietly admitted to a weakness, a lack of knowledge that he, Paul, the smart one, could help him overcome.

Timid at first, Paul's confidence multiplied as he drew an apparently absorbed Tyrone into his comfort zone of facts and figures. The next morning in class, Paul was surprised to find that Tyrone had shifted his stuff next to his, it looked permanent, and Paul got a lift from that. Over the ensuing days and weeks, they'd shared secrets, chuckled sotto voce and over time Paul felt drawn into Tyrone's sphere of influence and the immunity that came with it. He should have known there'd be a catch, but he wanted so much to belong he ignored the voices in his head and pushed back on the nagging doubts in the pit of his stomach. He'd found a friend.

Paul didn't mix well, studious, introverted, crap at sports and carrying a little too much weight, the girls ignored him, and the bullies singled him out. Humiliation was a slow burn that ate away at his confidence around his peers, so he buried himself in study.

Lessons had been his happy place, his sanctuary, but outside of learning his school days had been miserable, tolerated, something to get through, until Tyrone had sat beside him. Paul was as far from trendy and urbane as it was possible to be, geeky, friendless, and easy to beat up, but Ty had stopped the bullying, punched a few of his tormentors out, warned off others, raising Paul to an untouchable level.

A grateful Paul stuck to his new friend like glue, enjoying the security and freedom of being Ty's mate. The first time Ty had asked him to drop something off, just as a favour, Paul had been eager to please, keen to belong, and literally skipped off to do as bid. He'd delivered the package and Ty had rewarded him with a fist bump, £100 and a laddish promise that he'd get one of the girls he knew to sort out his virginity. He hadn't questioned what the parcel contained, anxious only to reinforce the friendship. The money had been an unexpected bonus, spent on a telescope.

The deliveries had become more frequent and insistent thereafter, the timings erratic, interfering with school, which was when the lying had started. At first his Mum and Dad had been pleased that he had begun making friends but lately, when the excuses for his poor school reports and attendance had become less convincing, they had started looking at him sideways whenever he opened his mouth.

Paul felt really bad about that; the mistrust that had developed at home. He could see in their faces that they couldn't understand where their little boy had gone or who this stranger was wearing his clothes, the hurt was evident. He wanted to tell them, wished he could, but confessing to them wouldn't alter the dynamic at school. Paul had no desire for a return to the norm, and they didn't have to live through his day.

If Paul stopped now, the fall from grace would be spectacular and humiliating. If Tyrone abandoned him; and he couldn't bear the thought of that so dependant had he become, there would be an explosion of pent-up bullying with Paul as the target.

Gradually, Paul had accepted his fate, suffered the slide, a dropping away of diligence, and at the same time an increase in the levels of fear his new activities induced. Ty had stopped asking and started demanding, had moved back to his customary workstation, leaving Paul in a grotesque limbo, isolated but still untouchable, provided he kept delivering. The message was clear, as long as he went along with it he was safe, still in the groove. There was no room for refusal.

Paul was painfully aware that he was trapped in a sequence of events from which he could see no way out, so he plodded on, ignoring the not-so-subtle sense of unease that was building within. Kidding himself it wasn't actually that bad, that he was being paid and that there was a sense of adventure attached, even a degree of importance, status. So, he didn't complain, accepted the cash, the security of Ty's patronage and cracked on.

It was worse for the girls. Early on, before the demands had started, Ty had said it was time to deliver on his promise and that tonight, Paul's virginity would be a thing of the past. He'd taken him to what he later heard described as a 'Trap' house. Essentially a shitty hovel where the dealers issued their instructions, users got high, stoned, or wasted depending on their preference, and the mules were herded.

Some of his contemporaries were female, the youngest looked to be around thirteen or so. He was told to pick one. Sex Ed classes informed gloomily of STD's and in the moment, this surfaced.

Faced with a choice between humiliation and selection, he reluctantly studied the options. He saw a lack of enthusiasm or hygiene, track marks, evidence of self-harm, runny noses, and glazed expressions.

At the back, sitting quietly and looking at her feet, was a frail blonde, perhaps slightly older than the other girls, who appeared relatively undamaged. He pointed a hesitant finger that felt like an accusation. Amid much back slapping and cheers of encouragement, he followed her up the stairs, a route she clearly knew. They sat together on the edge of a grubby, stained, unmade bed that reeked of use.

Now what? He'd asked. She'd said nothing, this wasn't her first rodeo, she knew the routine off by heart and started removing her top. He'd stopped her, he didn't know why, it just felt wrong and not how he'd imagined his first time would be. She'd looked up at him then and offered a resigned smile.

They'll know if we don't. I don't mind. Paul said no. It wasn't right. She'd shrugged and offered a weak smile repeating, *they'll know if we don't. It's the way things are.*

Paul, feeling a degree of influence for the first time in a long time, perhaps understanding that he was with someone with even less control over their own immediate future, offered an intelligent alternative. Her previously blank expression altered, shifted from passive acceptance to what may have been gratitude, he was pleased to see her smile.

They agreed to bounce on the bed for a minute or two and on a conspiratorial count of three, lifted from the bed and began the shared deceit. The bouncing prompted cheering from downstairs, and with that encouragement were almost laughing together as they increased the tempo, ran with it for a minute or two, then allowed it to subside, and stop. An almost perfect rendition of passion and exercise.

The noise from downstairs had matched their efforts and fell away to nothing as they rested. It was the last time Paul felt he'd had any control over events and their moment of rebellion forged more of a bond than any amount of meaningless sex.

Sitting side by side, putting off the moment when their 'lives' would have to resume, they opened up to each other. The girl had told him how she'd got involved. She was here to pick up drugs for *them*, wisely not specifying who *they* were. They had more in common than either of them had thought.

Apart from life at home, where Paul confessed he constantly worried about his deteriorating relationship with his folks; something the girl didn't have on her plate, their circumstances were similar, only their manner of entry and delivery of services differed. It was still slavery. She explained that what she was doing now or was supposed to have done with Paul had they carried it through, was how favours were done, how control was maintained. When she was finished here, she'd be picked up by a taxi and ferried back, essentially under guard, and wait until she was told what to do next. This was as good a place as any for her right now, at least she wasn't being abused.

Taking her cue, Paul embarrassingly admitted that this was supposed to be his passage into manhood, his "prize" for doing as he was told, but it just wasn't him.

They'd talked quietly about the dump they were in, the situation they were in, and Paul asked if there were a way out, *Not for us,* she'd said with a despair mirroring his own. They sat, knowing that their current sense of freedom was momentary, that soon they'd be right back where they were, neither wishing it were so.

He'd noticed the small badge she had pinned to her coat and, having an interest in Astronomy, recognised the profile of the constellation Libra. No, she'd said, it was a zodiac thing, that she was an air sign, intellectual and curious. They'd huddled while he explained the difference between astronomy and astrology, she put her hand to her mouth, amazed she'd been so dumb. He talked about the stars, how at night, he'd look up and dream. He had an app on his phone that told him what was above at any time. He opened it and pointed it skyward, his hand moving in a slow, gentle circle, coming to a halt as at that moment the International Space Station was orbiting overhead. They wished they were aboard.

Here, she'd said, unpinning the badge and fixing it to his jacket, *I want you to have this.* Shyly, he'd accepted saying he had nothing to offer in return. *No,* she'd said, *but there was something you could have taken, and didn't.*

Belatedly, Paul gave his name and asked for hers. *Lyla.*

Tonight was one of many train journeys he'd undertaken for whoever headed Tyrone's drugs gang and, whatever it was he was delivering, if he were caught with it, it would crash his world. Part of him longed for the anonymity of his old life, thinking that perhaps even the bullying would be preferable to this.

He thought that if he fought back, just once, it might stop, but knew that wouldn't happen. He determined again to enrol in self-defence classes but suspected that that wouldn't happen either. He looked out into the darkening evening. He knew he'd be late home, again, and the questions and shouting would start, that the lies would tumble out, easier in their repetition. He hated the game, knowing they knew something but he just…couldn't…tell.

From the darkness opposite the youth watched the station entrance, spotting the solitary, hesitant teenager instantly. This was his turf, or at least, that of his masters. He'd wait until the kid peeled away from the late evening commuters, most of whom were now headed for the station car park, then he'd job him.

Leon was buzzing, strutting with the new prestige that had been handed down. Yesterday he was just a younger, a falcon, the eyes, and ears of the gang, the lowest of the low in the hierarchy, right down at the bottom of the shit pile. But that was last week's news. He'd been told that this was his operation, all down to him, and he intended to make his mark.

A few days back, he hadn't even suspected he'd been noticed, but at last, after years of just scumming around on the rim, he was about to go large. He wouldn't fuck up. No way. So, as instructed, he'd travelled North, met the kid's handler, and dropped off the secure phone. He knew exactly when the kid was arriving and had worked out precisely what he intended to do. He wanted to move up, and this was his ticket to the top. The kid looked like plump, easy meat, he'd nail him, take the rucksack, and deliver. His rep would soar and the money would flow. He watched as the kid hung a left; cool, away from the illuminated frontage, but he needed to do him quick, before the meet.

The rucksack was on one strap over his right shoulder, Paul tried hard to remember the instructions he'd been given. Nothing was ever written down and he couldn't use the phone Ty had given him. It had no numbers stored in it and as he didn't know any he could reasonably call in the circumstances, it was reduced to the status of simply a receiving device.

But it did have a destination marked on an online map, a place for the drop off, he wavered, studying the picture, and shifting position, directed the phone left and right, trying to get it centred. Glancing anxiously down, an urgent desire to get this over with, the blue arrow eventually settled and pointed confidently to the left. Feeling it shift beneath his hand, he shrugged the rucksack into a more comfortable setting on his shoulder and walked away from the train station towards what the map showed to be a park of some kind.

Paul wasn't looking, checking his six, they called it, too intent following the arrow, a mission made more challenging because of his shaking hands. He tried to convince himself that the evening chill was the cause of his mad trembling, but the kidology failed; too bright not to extrapolate, he knew that he was out of his depth in every conceivable way.

At night, alone in his room, Paul's imagination gave him a proper working over, beating him up with a terrifying variety of possible scenarios, none of which ended well. Eventually, something would go wrong, and he'd be fucked. Part of him hoped that it would be the law that caught up with him first, rather than a screwed-up delivery or a lost consignment. He knew there was a painful and humiliating price exacted for failure and as the last link in the chain, he'd be the one to pay. His quieter, more comforting dreams saw him entering witness protection, finally being able to tell his parents of the living hell he had been going through, how he'd hated deceiving them, to be able to explain that this wasn't him, but the reality of his level of participation in what he now knew, courtesy of the internet, was a County Lines gang, wouldn't earn him another name, another town, another future. He was Paul, he'd always be Paul and he was petrified.

His tummy butterflied, starting a chain reaction of tremors that began as a tingle on his scalp, rolled through his substance, momentarily weakened his knees, and ended with the soles of his feet. There wasn't a single part of him that wasn't afraid. He mentally shook himself and resolved once again, for the umpteenth time since he'd become aware of his role as a drug mule, that as soon as he was seventeen he'd get out of this, even if it meant running away from home. He had a few years before that happened though and a lot could change before he made his getaway. He made the decision to start squirreling money away, and his hands steadied.

Even if he'd been street smart Paul was no match for the up and coming 'Younger' with iron in his hand. Leon knew he wouldn't hesitate, would jab hard, swift, deep, and multiple times. He'd seen it on TV often enough, studied the technique and reckoned the key was speed. He practiced in his room, feet spread for balance, the polished and sharpened knife cutting, gashing, and slicing through the air. He worked for hours, sweating, grunting, perfecting, dancing the dance.

This was Leons first job for the Albanian guys, but not his first time using a tool, he'd cut before, a simple bit of thieving that had gone south and he'd been forced to lash out with the blade. He'd breezed through it. The blood hadn't fazed him, if anything, he felt encouraged at the sight of it, an enemy down, out of the fight, he the victor, alive, hopping on the balls of his feet, eyes wide and white, exultant.

After that success and the fist bumps and high fives that came with it he made the easy decision to take his reputation to the next level. No-one here knew what this 'tourist' was capable of, and having seen him, faltering and uncertain, Leon knew he was the one, there'd never be one easier. The kid stank of vulnerability. If he 'queffed' this kid, killed him, they'd make him an 'Elder.' There'd be respect, guns, girls, drugs, and money, in that order.

But he also wanted a street name, *Leon* was just too pedestrian, he needed something cool to define him and at night, as he'd practiced with his blade, had figured out how best to get it. He'd work in a pattern. A special specific pattern. First the back of the neck; he knew this would put the kid on the floor, incapacitate him.

Hopefully, the kid would fall face first and then he'd work a design on the kids exposed back, going from bottom back to top, then down again, in a diamond pattern.

Diamondback had a ring to it, but maybe was a bit too long, they'd shorten it, perhaps to 'DB.' That wasn't gonna work, DB led too readily to Deadbeat and there was no way he was having that, then, it had come to him. He'd work the pattern on the kid, then later, would describe it as putting a diamond on the kid's back, then, as if it were an afterthought, say something like, *hey, isn't a diamondback a snake?* That's when he'd be christened. *Snake.*

His mind wandered further, settling first on a snake tattoo, then curved towards the prospect of reaching 18. He knew his cars, and when the time came, he'd get himself a Dodge Viper or an AC Cobra, the logo cementing the legend. Already, in his mind, he was sinuous, silent, deadly. He clenched his teeth together, emitting a quiet hissing sound.

He kept himself in the shadows, judging the kids' pace and lengthening his own, gradually making up the space between them, silent on his Reeboks. The kid was busy studying his phone, making occasional adjustments to his route. Leon knew where he was headed and timed his interception for a spot just inside the park, where the hedges rimming the green closed out the streetlights.

The kid went down when the knife pierced the back of his neck, a vigorous upward thrust that missed the spinal cord; its intended target, driving instead into the skull from beneath and violating the brain stem wherein dwells the medulla oblongata and pons, the regulating system for respiration.

Paul's world went black, and all breathing mechanisms ceased instantly. Snake couldn't know this but his next blow, separating the spinal cord and pushing through the kid's trachea was a wasted effort. Paul didn't need his windpipe anymore. What the knife did do was get stuck, a startling, unforeseen development that needed a knee on the twitching kids head to lever it out. Now the kid was down, he knelt quickly beside him and began what he hoped would become his trademark. It took a bunch of grunting and two-handed tugging to keep going. The knife not always sliding in as easily as anticipated, grating against the ribcage and some kind of suction offering resistance. Leon yearned for a gun and knew it had to be an automatic, a revolver hadn't the load he needed to paint his picture, six rounds did not a diamond make. A Glock 19 would do it with bullets to spare, he wanted a 19 real bad so kept stabbing.

Beneath the blows, Paul felt no pain, just a surreal sense of drifting, fading, ebbing. He had a brief premonition that this was the end of something, that this was how it was going to end. He was saddened by the notion that he was alone, that there were to be no heartbreaking farewells, no tears from his grieving parents.

The warmth he felt as he passed was a pool of blood, his, flowing and shielding him from the cold of the tarmac. Paul's journey ended much as it had begun, not understanding how it had come to this. His eyes closed, shutting out the place he'd never been before and the person he didn't know.

Paul was inert, defenceless, the process of dying beginning from the accidentally immaculate first strike, not feeling the remainder as his murderer stabbed studiously. The last sound Paul would make was involuntary, a weird leaking of air from his puncture wounds. Soon though, as his perforated respiratory system emptied, even that ceased. The same could not be said of Leon, who's breathing was hard, adrenalin fuelled, but eased as he finished his deadly motif.

He leaned back and looked down, checking for the first time since the neck stab that he'd got it about right. Birdlike, he cocked his head from left to right then, content with the image, wiped the knife on the bottom edge of the kids' jacket, like signing off, a Nike flourish he hadn't considered before but mentally added for the next time, thinking now that he should change the brand of trainers he habitually wore. Reebok was just letters, a name, but that careless wipe; he looked at it again, and using the tip of his knife, spruced up the outline.

Snapping the knife closed, Leon noticed a cool badge on the kid's jacket. It crossed his mind that a souvenir would be a good way of keeping count, so he took it, taking the time to pin it on.

He reached for the fallen rucksack, confirmed the contents, then smeared the outside with the kid's blood, blood he knew was very evident on his clothes and skin. When he got back to the trap house, he wanted to make an entrance, colour their world. The "Snake" would hatch.

LYLA

Lyla felt good, pumped. Most mornings they all ran together and then spent an hour either in the pool or the gym. The rest of her day would be spent either studying with Yvette, making up for the schooling she had missed in her previous life, helping Donna and Inga out in the animal sanctuary, or just hanging out with Sid in the summer house. She caught her breath sometimes, startled and amazed at how her life had changed. Not so long back, she'd have to fuck for food but here she was, trying to improve on her language skills, finding French a lot easier than Italian. La vie est belle. La vita e bella. Life is good. Mentally, she repeated the words, then spoke them out loud. She'd worked hard to 'lose' her regional accent, to become more cosmopolitan, and learning new languages helped in that. Sacha's American accent was especially glamorous and elements of that were easily adopted. Lyla rarely lapsed; she liked her new voice, her telephone voice. She was becoming anonymous, unidentifiable as the girl she was.

Once she'd dressed, she was headed for the Animal Sanctuary that Sacha had 'accidentally' created in the grounds of this spectacular home. She'd heard of unconditional love, some old disco song that sat on the edge of her memory, when her Mum had been around and in a rare, good mood for once. Until working with the animals though, it had been just that, a lyric. But those animals, the dogs especially, melted her heart, so much so that even doing the poo runs did not bother her, all part of the working day at the sanctuary. She felt like a person, not a piece of shit, something that resonated while picking up lumps of it. Later she'd read, socialise, perhaps watch some TV.

Sometimes she and Sacha would plan, plot, dream and laugh. They both had vacuum's that needed filling; each emotionally undernourished, one from loss, the other by casual neglect. While the generation gap was about right, both were aware that they were neither a substitute mother or a replacement daughter and while uncomfortable with the necessity, were at ease with the facts. Their relationship had developed into one where both were aware that they had responsibilities towards each other, but this was lightened by the flavour of their evolution into confidants, conspirators. She was grateful for the family that had found her rather than the one she'd been born with.

Tom on the other hand she was finding harder to get to know. He seemed content to maintain a smiling, hands off distance, not disinterested, but not fully engaged either, she couldn't put her finger on it but just felt that there was something holding him back. She hoped it wasn't personal, that it wasn't her, and then felt guilty for hoping that instead, it might just be the memory of a lost child.

She'd read somewhere that the bond between a father and daughter could be special; read it, never experienced it though. Though she knew she never would, part of her wanted to broach it with him, to tell him that she was not trying to be a replacement for his Ellen, that she was just trying to move forward and embrace her new life. And new was the simplest way to describe it, and as smart as she was becoming, she couldn't come up with a better word.

An afternoon on Sid's veranda had given her something to chew on; the old man's white hair and beard lending him the air of a prophet. *It's not you, love. It's a dad thing, he still reckons he should have had his little girls back, should have been there, kinda tough to live with, dontcha think? Give him time, he'll come round.*

Towelling her hair, Lyla stepped in front of the mirror and thumbed the switch on the drier. She gave herself an appreciative once over. She was a long way from Rochdale. Her skin was good, her naturally blonde hair glossy and tangle free. She ate well, slept well. She'd never felt fitter, stronger, or healthier.

Behind her, through the noise and the mirror, Lyla viewed her room. She'd asked if she could decorate it herself and was pleased with the result. Not necessarily at the quality of her efforts, unpractised with a brush and roller, but it now felt like hers, and that she belonged.

Sacha had said that this was as much her home as anyone else's and Lyla was beginning to feel it, to believe it and there was nowhere else she'd rather be. She pushed back any thoughts of the limitations that were imposed, knew that they were for her own safety and by extension, the safety of the group. She didn't fully understand much of what Sacha and the others were involved in and in truth, didn't much care other than that it seemed exciting, perhaps even a little dangerous, but in a good way. They were kind, nice people. Lyla had known proper shitheads from the other end of the spectrum and so was qualified to judge.

She dressed comfortably, a soft pair of tracksuit bottoms and a light indoor hoodie then sat at her desk, switching on her laptop. Lyla knew the rules, obeyed them, understood them, even. She could have the devices, go online, surf, whatever, provided she was anonymous, secure, didn't engage. An adjective and two verbs she thought, proudly. The education she was getting, courtesy of Yvette, kicking in. Rendering them wasn't a problem, in fact Yvette has been pleasantly surprised at how committed her student was and was working on accelerating the curriculum. Yvette wasn't the only one, Lyla reflected, with a smile. *Where did this come from? I thought I hated school.*

There was nowhere and no-one in her past she wished to revisit, so she didn't hanker for Facebook, X, Instagram, or any of the numerous social media platforms that inhabited the ether, her online history until recently was one of stupor and self-inflicted solitude. So, her laptop and phone were a self-policed educational tool and communication device, nothing more, nothing less. And she applied the rules of engagement rigorously.

She supposed she was scarred by her past but instead of thinking about it, dwelling on it, she pushed back, unwilling to be the victim she was intended or supposed to be. They were not going to win. She was. She used her harrowing past to spawn a belief in the future; one that hadn't really been fully discussed but the intimation was there. Despite the enforced breaks in her education, Uni was achievable. With the help of Yvette and some hard work, Sacha had hinted that she and Tom would see to the rest. Lyla wondered just how much Tom had been consulted on that, given the partial void that existed between them. As for the past, Sacha understood her curiosity and had agreed to her request, that she could monitor her local newspapers.

At first, she'd read avidly, noting with a grim smile that Faz and his mates had been reported missing and some arsehole politician had been caught with his pants down. She suppressed memories and anger, replacing them with thoughts of the future and optimism. Over time, rumour had become fact, the streets were being cleaned. The police were finally getting their act together and rounding up the predators. Opinion pieces howled belatedly; *how could this happen in our town?* Lyla knew the answer to that. *Nobody fucking cared.*

Today's news had a fresh bold banner complete with a picture of its subject. Something pulled at her, something deep and frightful. The name didn't come to her straight off the bat, but the image did. Immediately motionless, she read the text, then remembered.

Paul Cullen, his school photo headlining the article and staring out at her like a plea. Teenager stabbed. Frozen in place she read on, then, finding the purpose to move, unplugged her laptop, its battery power taking over as she went downstairs to the kitchen.

Sacha looked up as Lyla entered, her good morning smile evaporating.

"What is it, honey?"

Wordlessly, Lyla took the chair beside Sacha and placed the laptop front and centre.

Sacha pulled it closer and studied the page.

"You knew him?"

Lyla nodded, close to tears.

Placing an arm around the distressed girl, Sacha read on.

Paul Cullen, 15, had been found stabbed to death in the park of a coastal town. There'd been no explicable reason for him being there, but evidence pointed towards some kind of low-level involvement in the County Lines phenomenon.

Sacha closed the lid and sat quietly alongside her ward, she knew Lyla well enough to know that when she was ready, when she could or wanted to, she'd speak. Meanwhile, she'd offer what silent comfort she could. She could feel the tension in Lyla's shoulders, the suppression before the unavoidable moment of telling. Lyla sagged beneath her, and the words came.

"He was a bit younger than me, a couple of years I think but he was the only one who ever showed me any respect or kindness."

Sacha never asked Lyla for details, aware that when the time was right, she'd either open up on her history, or wouldn't. Since her rescue the girl had been surprisingly balanced and resilient, but the shell would crack one day, and Sacha was resolved to be there when it did. Today, it seemed was that day.

She listened as Lyla told the story of how together they'd conspired to cheat their respective masters, of that tiny moment of joy she'd experienced during the years she'd been a pawn. The one time she could remember smiling and, in the telling, she felt ashamed.

"I'd forgotten all about him, like I try to forget everything."

"And you're remembering now?"

Lyla nodded. She'd gotten out of the habit of crying, but it returned now with the memory of the boy who for a brief time, had taken nothing when he could have had the only thing she had left to offer. Through her misery she haltingly told the little she knew.

The County Lines thing was on the periphery of Sacha's knowledge, gleaned mostly and abstractedly from the media. From what she'd just read, the police statements and newspapers conclusions seemed to tie in with what little she did know.

"D'you think the article is accurate?"

"Must be, on his own? Miles from home? Burn phone? Been there, done that."

The recall had placed an edge to Lyla's voice, her hometown accent briefly resurfacing. Sacha knew better than to probe so she simply hugged the girl a little tighter. The moment passed and Sacha sensed a question forming, a bracing of the shoulders that signalled resolve.

Raising her head, Lyla looked Sacha straight in the eye. "You know I know that you and Tom don't exactly have a nine to five job, right?"

From that first meeting at Lyla's old school, Tom and Sacha posing as something they weren't, masked men in the night. Spook tech, violence, guns, a wild pursuit across Turkey. Lyla had witnessed all that and more, with only the briefest of explanations asked for or offered.

"I guess so." Sacha conceded. Too much had happened for Lyla to be oblivious.

"Can you guys look at this? Punish someone? I know a name, Tyrone."

Sacha concentrated hard on her answer. They'd taken this girl out of that world and putting her back in it, even by proxy, would be a retrograde step. Lyla was doing brilliantly, achieving, mending. Sacha sensed that trust mattered here, no promises that might be broken could be made but some steps could be taken, perhaps even had to be, closure took many forms, she knew.

"Those sorts of decisions are above my pay grade, honey. But yeah, we can take a trip to the big house. I'll make the call."

"And" ...Lyla hesitated, knowing it was a big ask. "I would really like to go to the funeral."

PAGING AWAY

Since making the local news, though no drugs were found on his body, the presence of a burn phone was widely reported, and a natural assumption made that he'd been moving drugs around. There would be no grand send off, a sense of shame and misunderstanding infiltrating proceedings.

The police had been surprisingly sympathetic, explaining that Paul was a victim, not just of a violent, fatal attack, but of the County Lines phenomenon. The Support Officer they'd been assigned had sat with his parents and gently explained the nature of the beast and had they had been made aware of Paul's involvement he wouldn't have been prosecuted but safeguarded. This knowledge served only to sharpen the pain Paul's parents were already feeling.

The SO knew what was going through their minds, she'd been here so many times before, that they should have known their quiet, studious boy could not have turned into a delinquent, that there would have been an explanation.

Then the second guessing began; why didn't they push harder, question the signs that were right under their noses, if only they had tried harder the outcome might have been different, they had failed their only son.

Even though Paul's parents now had a partial explanation for their boy's makeover from student to miscreant, they had no answers as to how. A teacher had pointed a finger at a known troublemaker, Tyrone, but with the keen instinct of the guilty, he'd gone off the radar and hadn't been seen since the news broke about Paul's murder.

As he hadn't had much in the way of friends, Paul's funeral was limited to family and the few narcissistic classmates that alleged intimacy. However bogus, their mourning would feature on their social media platforms as a visible manifestation of their nobility in adversity and they would be consoled, special. Virtue signalling was now a competitive sport.

Dressed as they were in street clothes, and preoccupied as the small formal gathering at the bottom of the hill was, Tom, Sacha, Sid, and Lyla were simply part of the backdrop.

Their attention was on a small group of subdued schoolchildren waiting restlessly on the astroturf surrounding a freshly dug grave at the bottom of the slope, some distance from where they stood. Shuffling, inattentive, you could tell by their demeanour that none of them really wanted to be there, but Paul was a classmate, and dead, a tragedy. 'Standing with Paul', on Facebook in co-opted victimhood would look cool and there was always the chance of shedding a tear on TV, breathless, sobbing, social consciences polished. That, and it got them out of classes for a couple of hours. Paul had been friendless in life, less so, it appeared, in death, there was an ersatz, emotionless quality to the gathering.

Sacha stood hand in hand with Lyla. Tom, and Sid sentinels, silent at their backs. The flowers in Lyla's free hand were a common sight, the cemetery sparsely populated by attentive figures, some knelt, weeding, brushing, paying tribute, while in the middle distance roamed a tombstone tourist with a camera.

Lyla tensed, gripping harder on Sacha's hand as a hearse rolled sombrely into view, behind it, a single black limousine. She felt Sid's touch as a comfort on her shoulders. This wasn't the first procession they'd seen today but the assembly around the grave had announced its arrival as particular. The cars stopped and a tail suited man with a top hat and cane exited the hearse and led the cortege on foot to the graveside.

At the back of his mind, Tom recalled this as an old tradition, paging away, the cane known as a wand, the knowledge stemming from the second worst day of his life, laying Ellen to rest. His head dropped as he blanked out the live scene he'd witnessed at the cottage in Devon, trying to repress the memory. An adult, most likely a teacher, herded the class in a semi-circle, their backs to Lyla. A grinning youth, a baseball cap worn backwards, took a selfie. Behind the hearse, a hunched, desolate woman was helped from the limousine, a man supporting her, evidently Paul's parents, as was.

A priest, eerily invisible until now, took up the customary position as the coffin was slid from the belly of the hearse, lifted, and borne to its final resting place. The service, even from their distant viewpoint, was an awkward blur. Only the children present and their teacher knew each other. Pauls parents stood alone. In the back of her mind Lyla was thinking two things; that if her life had not changed this could have been her and would her parents have come out of the woodwork to bury her. Bleakly, she thought not, unless someone set up a crowd funding page.

The service was mercifully short, and the cortege was on a schedule. Less than 30 minutes after being populated, the graveside was clear. Tom placed a hand on Lyla's shoulder.

"Wait." He said softly, sadly recalling the final act of Ellen's entombment. "It won't be long."

In the distance, a JCB coughed into life, a small, black cloud rising from behind a screen. Emerging, it crabbed to the grave and began to back fill, finishing with a shovel blade smoothing the packed earth. It toiled noisily off, leaving behind a silence punctuated only by startled birdlife.

"We can go down now."

Wordlessly, Lyla nodded and led the way, her flowers cradled. There wasn't much in the way of floral tributes, just one purportedly from classmates and the other, from his parents, taken from the hearse.

Lyla knelt, she'd bought pink roses, having read that they were a Libran's favourites. They'd never discussed birthdays, not in the short time they'd had together, but she remembered the badge she'd given him and the evident pleasure he took from it. Regaining her feet, she stood silently, gazing down at the brown scar in the green.

Sacha moved to her side and placed a consoling arm on her shoulder, waiting quietly as the girl seemed lost in contemplation. After a time, she felt compelled to intervene.

"Are you ok, honey?"

Lyla nodded. "I was just talking…in my head…saying goodbye."

"We ought to leave." Said Sid, mindful of their circumstances. "We don't want to attract attention."

Lyla turned, facing them. Her face tear stained but grim.

"We're going to find who did this, right?"

Tom frowned; he didn't like the sound of *we*.

As much as he had come to care for Lyla, and despite himself, he did, he was very aware that they hardly knew her and as happy as he was that Sacha had carved out a new role for herself with the girl, to Tom she was an unknown quantity. Sacha caught the alarm in his expression.

She gripped Lyla's arms, gently but firmly. "We'll talk to the big house. If they look into it and find anything, be sure of one thing. It won't be us or them that deal with it. This is for the Police to take care of."

At the trap house, the loss of the consignment was taken as an occupational hazard and in the absence of any evidence to the contrary; no-one knew who'd taken it, they turned the setback into a warning. Putting the word out that it had been them who'd 'sorted' Paul. Paul had been unwilling, a bad choice, a pussy. A knife was produced and waved around threateningly. *Don't be like Paul.* It said. Life went on.

ALTIN

The apartment stank of shit, unwashed bodies, and stale cigarettes. It was a needle, spoon, and foil littered pigsty in a high rise they'd cuckooed from the junkie tenant, a drug debt laden crackhead currently spaced out in a side room. Its decoration consisted of dripping wallpaper and faded paintwork cracking from wormed skirting and doors. Discarded food lay stale, mouldy and rotting on every flat surface, furniture stuffing bulged from ripped, filthy cushions, a stained mattress decorated a corner, there was the potential for contracting dysentery just from breathing the air. But it had electricity, power needed for the blenders and presses that repackaged the cocaine. And that space was relatively clean.

Whenever possible, Altin avoided coming to these places, it was hazardous for a man in his position, but the risk was worth the reward. There was a job here that he acknowledged could be entrusted to others, but in these cases, he much preferred to be hands on.

Kosovo. Ethnic cleansing. He missed the war and the opportunities it had presented, particularly the exploitation of the vulnerable and defenceless. Since adolescence, he'd had an appetite for rape, seeing something he liked and simply taking it, appealing to his sense of privilege. Romance was overrated he thought, involving courtship and an emotional investment, an extravagance that required empathy. There was no need for this in wartime, he could do as he pleased with no fear of judgement or retribution, and he'd made the transition from rape to murder with ease. But with familiarity, comes contempt, supplanted in time with boredom.

Casting around for more sophisticated fulfilment, he'd taken to cutting. After all, they belonged to him now. They'd had to be nailed or tied down, their resistance a distraction. Thrusting his hands into the fresh open wounds, his fingers would probe, seeking out movement within, the stuff of life. He had held a beating heart in his hands, was feeling and watching it fail, and with that came an epiphany. That the muscle he held was the difference between life and death for everyone and in that, there was value, and where there is value, there is the potential for profit.

So, midst the chaos of the war and the suspension of humanity that came with it, he'd begun harvesting organs as a sideline. With the recruitment of a compliant and well rewarded surgeon he'd become an expert, if unqualified, anaesthetist. But the open market had a specific requirement. The goods could not be damaged, requiring that he finesse his technique and with time and practice he'd learned to keep them alive whilst his surgeon reaped the valuable body parts. Kidneys were his personal favourite. He knew that a heart was only viable for four to six hours once outside the body, the kidney though, if packed properly, could last for as long as thirty-six hours. Kidneys had a further advantage in that the people that had the money to destroy their own, were the best placed to pay to skip the queue. It was a first world problem, high blood pressure, diabetes, indications of an indulgent lifestyle and a healthy bank balance. He had little interest in the group that were unfortunate enough to inherit or develop kidney disease, he wasn't a charity, this was business with a little pleasure thrown in. He enjoyed studying, observing, sitting quietly beside them during the harvest. He liked to hold their hands, taking them close to death, then the god like revival process, keeping them breathing just long enough to ensure that they delivered fresh goods to market. But when the cutting was done, when the nod above the mask had been given, when they had nothing left that he wanted, he'd shift in his chair and initiate the wind down process. He'd taken to feeling the wrist for the ebbing pulse, watching as the light in their eyes faded then went out, made attempts at bringing them back, some exhilaratingly successful, some depressingly not, but they all ended the same way. *In another life,* he thought, *I might have been a vet.*

It had been a long time since the end of the war. His stomach shifted in anticipation; hunger stirred.

He sniffed the air with distaste, preferring the cleanliness and energy of his legitimate businesses, particularly the gym's. He was here to close this place down having already acquired another in a different neighbourhood, nowhere was secure for long, not in this business. The comings and goings of low life's attracted attention, and Altin was no attention seeker, at least not in this aspect of his work. He stood out here though, surrounded by addicts, shitty furnishings, mildewed walls, and sticky carpets, he'd need to be quick.

Long hours on a press bench and punch bag had earned him a classic, sculpted, V shaped torso. He was tall, tanned, dark haired, brown eyed and together with his requirement for meticulous grooming, was high on the Adonis index. The other inhabitants of the room were less blessed, Altin did not use his own products, his Oompah Loompas though, when finished weighing and packing, were allowed to scrape the tables and liquidisers. What they did with the powder after that was of no concern to him, they could sell it, though most were likely to use it. Altin's employment package was generous compared to most.

Altin's journey to power had been planned and careful. The war was over, their income stream restricted, new pastures must be explored and exploited. So, he'd left Albania privately on an AquaStar Ocean Ranger provided by his brother for one specific purpose; get into England and build. He'd floated luxuriously to Italy across the Ionian Sea, been met in the moonlight by a sleek, black, Lexus which over the course of 2 lazy days, took him to Calais. There he'd dumped his identity, changed his clothes, and joined a crowded dinghy across the English Channel. The rest was a carefully documented history. Altin was a poster boy for the immigration liberals.

He'd done well as a recent illegal, followed the rules, got the papers and the legitimacy that went with them, started small but now had two-night clubs and a string of gym's spanning the South Coast. But that's where the legitimacy ended. Altin had spent a considerable amount of time touring the area finding the businesses he needed and once found, one way or another, by fair means or foul, they were going to be his.

He'd acquired them using methodology, by intimidation at first and if that failed, with casual violence. Out of courtesy, he'd first send an anonymous warning. He knew from experience that this first approach would be met with disdain and would need to be followed up with a little rape here and there. His personal preferences aside, he knew daughters made too much noise after the event, so he'd been shrewd, taking a wife or mother from time to time, their shame and his verbal threats issued during the act with the promise of worse to come ensuring eventual compliance. There were other levers he could and did pull until eventually, his targets saw reason. He always paid market price, he was nothing, if not fair.

Once acquired, the businesses were improved and propped up by the profits of his family's real trade. From a well-crafted distance, and with some contempt, he'd observed the stupidity of others. Rival, city-based gangs posting supremely idiotic You Tube videos displaying wealth, arrogance, weapons, and identities. *No.* Bujar, his brother had said. *Make no waves, be invisible. You will be our 'Krye,' in Britain.*

And it had worked beautifully, he was the Boss, his family ties backed up by a personal penchant for violence securing him the position, his preference for a low profile maintaining it. It irked him in a small way that he rarely played any part in direct action. He missed the deep gut thrill of power over life and death, today's rare and risky outing the exception.

Altin glanced across the room, his eye on the new kid. A denim shirt open to the waist showed an underdeveloped chest, more bone than muscle, but on it, and the true purpose of the open shirt, was displayed a fresh tattoo, some kind of serpent. Leon caught his glance and, eager to illustrate his usefulness and elevated status, bustled busily on new, white Nikes amongst the mixers and packers, checking weights and measures. His eyes flicked up nervously, looking for approval. Altin gave it, a slight nod sufficient.

The youth, Leon, he remembered had been sent to intercept a courier. The result had been messy but had sent a warning. Stay away from my territory. Altin was unconcerned about the murder or the manner in which it had been arranged and carried out. The English were soft, stupid, complacent. At first, he'd been amazed to find their police went largely unarmed, a posture which placed them at an immediate disadvantage to his own organisation.

He got his arms in with the drugs, on the Balkan route, both were cheap and plentiful, originating in Afghanistan and trafficked by Bujar, though since the Taliban crackdown on the poppy growers he'd moved away from opium and was now a specialist cocaine importer, Ecuador his favoured source.

He watched the tables as the new consignment was split and weighed into resale packages. Altin didn't cut it though he knew some low-level dealers further down in the chain did. He was unconcerned at that, it was still purer than the Brits were used to, and he priced it right, well below the traditional levels. His was the Woolworths of the drug world. Pile it high, sell it cheap, blow away the competition.

The repackaging complete, Altin gave the order to clear up the paraphernalia and move on with it to the next site. As the last of the walking inhabitants left and closed the door behind them, Altin slipped on a pair of surgical gloves, took the hypo from his jacket pocket, and high with anticipation, went into the bedroom. The hippie was still out of it. Altin slapped him, shook him to some level of awareness, it was important that the eyes, the window to the soul, were open.

"Wake up, my friend. I have a gift for you."

Altin held up the syringe, offering it. The psychonaut focussed, his pupils dilating. Altin noted they were an attractive shade of grey and a saw a backlight come on as what was left of his brain registered what was on offer. Holding out an arm, he sighed gratefully and gave a weak, cracked lip smile.

Altin looked down at the exposed chest and abdomen and wished for the freedom to use a knife, but that would initiate an unwelcome investigation. He sighed with regret, having to be satisfied with simply observing the process rather than profiting from it. Those days were gone.

Neither were concerned about infection, so no swabbing was asked for or offered. Gently, avoiding numerous track marks and old vascular damage, Altin tapped for a vein. Finding one that wasn't in the process of collapsing, Altin delivered the overdose, heroin cut with fentanyl. He sat, his fingers resting gently on the junkie's wrists, almost sensing the dopamine release through the skin, a little sweat, some heat.

Experience told him what to expect next and leaning down he peered closer, deep into those grey eyes which, as the pulse became thready, lost focus, then, as the beat beneath his fingertips finally ceased, the cornea, aqueous humour and lenses grew opaque as they lost their sensitivity to light, flattening, finally, dead. Altin breathed, unaware that somewhere along the way, he'd stopped. Sighing, he placed the hypo in a dead hand, fingerprints carefully arranged.

Altin left, he had an appointment at the gym.

AMES

From the enveloping warmth of his office, Ames watched as in the distance, Bailey and the boys went through their regime. At 55, he envied them their relative youth. He knew the routine; whatever the weather, they challenged each other on their fitness levels. Today was summer turning to autumn, and began as always, with a run around the estate.

They'd created a punishing circuit, elements of which had been turned into a 'Mudder.' The last 400m was inevitably a race, the winner generally determined en route, skulduggery usually the deciding factor. As the last man crossed the line, they formed a steaming huddle then broke off and headed towards his building.

While they were en route, Ames considered the makeup of the group. Mid to late thirties, they were all ex-SF in one form or another, Bailey, a Reconnaissance Regiment veteran and the only female, a first-class analyst and IT virtuoso. James and Ollie, he classed as the originals. Their background was vague, but Ames knew enough to safely assume they were former SAS or SBS. One day, he might even ask. They had been Christian's personal security detail from Day One, long before Ames had been recruited and presented with Themis as an idea.

Dave and Neil, an ex-para, and Royal Marine respectively, were later recruits. Operations had exposed deficiencies in the unit, and it had become clear that special skill sets were needed, they provided them.

Dave had a way of procuring prohibited items. Mentally, Ames gave his head a wobble and said it how it was, Dave acquired arms, and this was England, where possession of any deadly weapon was tightly controlled. Quite how he got them or where from were not questions a man of Ames law enforcement background was prepared to ask. But guns, munitions, explosives, and all manner of strictly military paraphernalia were now available, if or when needed.

Neil's talents sat easier with Ames. A skilled mechanic and master of improvisation, he adapted and maintained their growing fleet of vehicles. As a whole, they were now what he officially considered the core of his team.

Then there was Adey, immersed in his trade and seemingly oblivious to life outside the compound, he multi tasked as their forensics analyst, chemist; essentially anything to do with test tubes, centrifuges, and Bunsen burners. His role was firmly set as civilian support and deniable. He'd been found in a pathology lab, overqualified and under used and had grabbed at the chance of his own research facilities and a generous salary in exchange for advice, analysis, and discretion. Of late, Adey had developed an enthusiasm for some of their left field requests, always exceeding expectations.

On the periphery, were Tom and Sacha Hood, currently at their home, settling the girl, Lyla, in. Lyla was a by-product of breaking up the grooming gang. Then there was Sid, a taciturn Australian of indeterminate vintage. All Ames really knew about him he'd gleaned from the boys who were oddly deferent to the old man. SF from at least a generation ago, Sid lived a hippy like existence in the old summer house in Tom and Sacha's garden.

The past months since the Turkey operation had been largely uneventful, James and Ollie, in need of something to do, had resurrected Task Force Echo and had been filling in their time by tormenting the numerous dealers and pushers that infected schoolchildren. The dealers' methods were consistent and uniform, only the names and places changed, so James and Ollie maintained their tried and tested technique. Identify, disrupt, humiliate where possible. Never in one place for too long, they roamed the UK with their brand of rough justice and a ladybird stamp. He'd need to have a word about that. The media had noted the trend and were beginning to ask questions. It was all well and good subtly commemorating a lost child, but a risk of exposure came with their unique modus operandi.

Setting that concern aside, Ames considered ring rust. The unit was becoming isolated from one another, scattering into their own specific roles, and becoming insular. He'd need to find them a team tasking job soon, something to get the juices flowing and unify the group. It was that, or face being dragged from his office and compelled to join the morning ritual. Ames was not a runner. That said, he was a team player, and left his office for the kitchen; the guys would be hungry for breakfast.

The sharp end of the organisation all lived on site, each having an apartment within the old mansion. It made life simpler, adding cohesion to the unit, almost barracks like, a latter-day Bletchley Park.

During downtime, James seemed hellbent on a full refurbishment of what was once a beautiful building, elements of it having been allowed to deteriorate under MOD ownership. He'd asked for and been granted a free hand and could often be seen wandering around with tape measures and colour charts, lost in the world of interior design. He'd gone so far as to build his own woodworking shop in an annex, all he needed now was a spray booth and he would be away. Ames had heard mumblings that his current project was the resurrection of the disused Billiard Room, there was even talk of a bar installation. Ames liked that idea, he wasn't one for socialising but if it had to be done, then it should be amongst friends.

For two men as close as James and Ollie were, they couldn't have been more different. Perhaps that's what made it work. Where James was tidy, organised, creative, Ollie's personal admin was a shambles and much to James's dismay, his quarters were a borderline squat. If he was passionate about anything, it was that bloody Triumph Spitfire that littered the parking area. No-one had a reserved bay and as a consequence, there were oil stains in all of them.

When not operational, Neil would be in the garage workshop, adding horsepower and gadgetry to the motor pool, while Dave could be found in his own fiefdom with the smell of hot oil, metal shavings, drills, and lathes. The occasional loud bang accompanied by a shouted 'Sorry!' and rising black smoke, rattled windows and nerves but no one asked exactly what he was doing, some things it was better not to know. It was an anarchical 'Q' Department, both men in their element.

Tom, Sacha, and Lyla visited from time to time, Lyla having struck up quite a relationship with PC. Peter Christian, the stockbroker who financed the group and occupied the top floor. It seemed that Lyla, having known isolation when in the hands of the grooming gang, sensed a kindred spirit in the man upstairs and had made it her mission to bring him back to the land of the living. They took long walks together and PC, to the surprise of everyone and Tom's relief in particular, was teaching her to drive, the estate perfect for the purpose.

“Morning Boss.” James, rosy from the run and a shower had wandered in and grabbing a sandwich and a coffee, took a seat at the large, melamine dining table.

“Morning. Who won?”

“Bailey. Again.”

“You lot need to try harder or stop ambushing each other on the way round.”

James smiled. “It’s just a fitness thing, Boss, with a hint of jeopardy thrown in. You ought to join us.”

“Oh, I will, James, just as soon as I’ve bought a bicycle.”

James smiled. Ames’s sense of humour was developing nicely, which was, in itself, a nice development.

“Anything new?”

“Just some info on progress up north. We’ll wait for the others, and I’ll fill you in.”

“Tom ‘n that are due today, I’m told.”

“They are.” Replied Ames. “They’re apparently on their way back from a funeral and have something they’d like to discuss, also Lyla wants to tear around the estate. Fingers crossed Neil’s repaired the sacrificial car since her last visit.”

In ones and two's, the last of the group entered the kitchen until all were present and had finished breakfast, snippets of conversation and banter passing between them as the tables were cleared for the briefing.

"Right." Said Ames. "I've got an update from Turkey and another from Arham."

Arham Khan, the deeply frustrated policeman whose phone call had set in motion the destruction of the grooming gang.

"The investigation into half a dozen bullet ridden cars at the bottom of a Turkish ravine isn't achieving much. They can't identify the individual we know to be Badboy, but he had no dependents so is of no interest to us. Faz though, courtesy of a false passport he was carrying, has been identified and declared dead. This free's up his family to gain access to his assets so financially they'll be fine. I'd like to believe that emotionally the same applies. Gerry and Mo haven't surfaced so for the time being we'll assume they came to a sticky end, and it seems that Urquhart isn't missed; his contractors are carrying on as normal and he had no family to speak of. Mo's taxi firm is now clean, as far as we can make out, and his wife and kids are benefiting from its continued operation. We can reasonably assume they don't miss him either so, overall, a satisfactory outcome. Mayfield has been forced to resign and is currently under arraignment."

No-one had wanted any collateral damage though some was inevitable. They could live with the minimal effects their operation may have had on the innocent.

"Arham is now heading up a dedicated and generously funded national task force aimed at these gangs, trawling over old reports, complaints and the like and following them up. Given the scale of abuse and the authorities earlier off handed treatment of it agencies are fully co-operating and arrests are being made, and not just of groomers. Their facilitators are being rounded up. How far up that is allowed to go before someone puts the brakes on is anyone's guess but for now, let's put that in the plus column."

"How are the girls?"

"Morning, Bailey. By all accounts, fine, though one of them is not doing as well as the others."

A chorus of "Libby!" met the remark.

"Yes. That's the one. Sandra hopes to work her problems out with her, but she doesn't seem to want what's on offer. It seems Libby actually misses her old life, I'm told she absconds on a regular basis, but Sandra isn't giving up on her."

"Good luck with that." said Ollie.

"So, what's next?" James asked.

"We consolidate." Replied Ames. "Dave and Neil have plenty to do in the workshop and armoury, dull but necessary, Bailey tells me there are systems she wants to put in and I'd like you two," Ames looked at James and Ollie, "to give me some Bunker time."

"Really?" Replied Ollie, always keen to be hands on.

Ames nodded. "It's clear that we're not always going to be able to achieve our aims within the usual constraints. If Turkey taught us one thing it's that guns are easily available and the oppositions desire to use them is plain. If they are prepared to use deadly force, we all, and I include me, need to be proficient."

James raised an eyebrow. Ames had been specifically opposed the use of arms unless absolutely necessary. Ames noticed the query.

"I'm a realist, James. And I don't want to find myself in a situation where my shortcomings impact on the group. I want to be brought up to standard."

James nodded. Ollie spoke. "Cool."

The debrief over, Ames asked James into his office for a solo session. Sitting, James waited. He wasn't one to pre-empt what was either a speech or a lecture. He was wrong on both counts; this was a chat.

"Can we talk about Ollie?"

"Ollie? What about him?"

Ames didn't need a loose cannon on deck and had questions about Ollie, doubts that needed settling.

"This casual, offhand attitude of his, is it just a way of dealing with things? PTSD, perhaps?"

"You're worried, Boss. About Ollie?"

Ames nodded. He knew next to nothing about these boys' previous activities. No psyche report, no discharge papers, honourable or otherwise. All he had was what was in front of him. He believed that morally, their compasses were set about right, experience told him that. He also believed that of the two of them, James seemed the most well-adjusted, so here he was, probing.

James got it, this was the dance. He'd been military as long as he could remember, both as a child, moving around with his folks, and as an adult, joining as early as he could. Ollie's story wasn't exactly parallel, but it wasn't far off. James particularly understood the mystique surrounding Special Forces, of which they'd both been a part. Civilians and operators both struggled, one to understand, the other to be understood. Perhaps they should've written a book.

James knew that the policeman misinterpreted Ollie's attitude, Ollie appeared to be a cynic, he wasn't, he seemed casual with violence, again, he wasn't, he seemed quicker to act than to think, again, not so. James knew this. Perhaps it was time Ames knew also.

"We were on an Op, two teams of two, where or when isn't important, except that it was dangerous on a level most won't understand. Me'n Ollie were on a hillside, with a second team on a hill opposite, all of us looking at a farmhouse set at the bottom of a valley. We'd been there about ten days, hiding, watching, scratching, freezing, wet and knackered; two hours on, two hours off takes it out of you. We had intel that an arms drop was scheduled but all we saw was regular farm stuff and were thinking of standing down and getting back into the warm. But on what we figured would be our last night, there was unusual and worrying activity, some arsehole used IR against us."

Ames raised an eyebrow.

"Infra Red." James clarified. "Not usually found in an agricultural community."

It had been a while since Ames had heard of the use of Infra-Red, technology had moved on, Thermal Imaging and the like, the operation James was describing was clearly one from way back.

"Our passive IR detector was a standard bit of kit that usually sat there and did bugger all, we used to gripe about the extra weight, batteries and the like but not that night and never since. It got a bit noisier, and I can tell you that at this point, we were both wide awake.

The detector was going nuts, so we switched it off. We could hear the undergrowth being searched, like grouse being flushed out, and the beaters had numbers. Ours arses were hanging out in the breeze, we couldn't bug out, comms were shit, and there was nowhere to go, nothing to do except sit, watch, wait and hope. And it's the waiting that gets to you. We knew the risks and the consequences of being caught. Crucifixion was a local favourite; a handy tree was nearby, and I remember eyeing it up. This went on all night, and I mean, all night. They missed us by only a couple of feet more than once. You could smell 'em. We lay in that hide, back-to-back, waiting for the bad news. We'd already decided months before that we weren't going to be captured so if we got compromised there was only one option, and surrendering wasn't on the list. Eventually morning came. The hillside was quiet again, no indication that whatever had gone on in the night had actually happened, but down in the valley on the farm, the routine had changed, patterns altered, but why wasn't clear. We couldn't be certain of anything other than someone had been out all-night cleaning house, looking for the likes of us. Ollie had the best optics, a sniper rifle, so whatever happened next was entirely his call. Now remember, we'd been shitting ourselves for hours, hadn't slept, we knew something was up, we were wet, exhausted and in the mood for a fight. If we got into one it was up to Ollie's judgement, nothing else, no tech, no intel, just a Mk1 human brain. And something else," James leant forwards, adding emphasis, sharing a secret.

"If he made the wrong call, we had ways of making it right, no-one was going to jail, not for a combat decision and pulling a trigger is delivering a non-negotiable verdict. Anyway, I waited, expecting a shot at any moment and a body to drop down at the farm. Nothing happened. Ollie took the rifle from his shoulder and shook his head. Our farmer put something in his car and drove away."

"That's it? That's your story?"

"Not quite, Boss. That car got stopped down the road and searched and I mean, searched. It was just a bundle of tools, nothing more, it turned out our intel was bilge that day, the guy was just a farmer, nothing more. Now Ollie could easily have taken that shot, I know I wanted to, wound so tight as we were and doing nothing felt like a huge let down, but later, after the exfil, I asked him what it was that stopped him pulling the trigger. *I couldn't be sure.* Was all he said.

"And your point?"

"Pulling a trigger is easy, there's nothing simpler, just exercise a muscle or two and it's done. He might even have got a medal. But the thought process is what's important. He later said it was the best shot he'd never made. He'll kill if he has to, but he's a soldier, not some grinning maniac."

James paused again, recalling Ames initial query.

“You mentioned PTSD. Who knows? Between the two of us there’s enough history to make the claim. There’re times he’s turned up for wet work wearing skull masks and all kinds of weird shit. He makes bad jokes, gives the impression of craziness, he’s the worst guy I know to stand next to at a funeral, you never know what’s going to come out of his mouth but that’s just his way of dealing with it. Laughing at death, or even with death is his coping mechanism. He aint the first and he won’t be the last to deal with stuff that way. But our business is full of people who judge without using their judgement, sometimes just for the hell of it, for the emotional release, as I might have done after that night on that hillside. I wouldn’t have spent the last ten years working with a guy that didn’t think about what he was doing. I trust him to make the right calls and I ignore whatever camouflage he puts up.”

“Did you ever find out what all the IR and bush beating was about?”

“Nope. Later analysis decided it was a ‘come on’, false intel designed to get folk like us on task, isolate us and take our heads. The Int guys said we were lucky. I’d argue that we were well trained, professional, but mostly cool under pressure. We could have exploded out of that bush, put a shitload of munitions downrange and likely have got away with it. But that’s how it is most of the time. That farmer was involved in some way but on that day, when his car was searched, he was clean. It bugs Ollie, he wonders what that farmer went on to do that could have been prevented if he'd taken him out, but you can't second guess every decision, you just have to live with the one's you make. I'll tell you what though, that farmer, if that's what he actually was, was one brave bastard, setting himself up like that. You have to respect that kind of courage, if nothing else, it makes you warier of your enemies."

After James had left, Ames sat at his desk, pensive, a little wiser, and grateful that he was on the same side as those two.

SO, IT BEGINS.

Lyla sat in Bailey's office, her laptop open, staring wordlessly at the face on the screen. Paul, pretty much as she remembered him.

She was restless, resentful at being left out of whatever was going on in what she now knew was a briefing room. The 'adults' were in there talking about Paul, *her* Paul, having a conversation she desperately wanted to be involved in, should be involved in, and a knotty, complex angst had her torn between her love and loyalty for to Sacha, Tom, and a deep fondness for the group as a whole, and the need to know more about how Paul had come to be a newspaper headline and the desire to do something about it.

She felt a surge of anger as she thought about Tyrone. She'd known about him, of course, the whole school had. And if she was going to find out how and why Paul had died, Tyrone was the link; the very obvious first step. Her problem wasn't whether she should go, she mostly knew the answer to that, but the last thing in the world she wanted to do was disappoint her new family and friends.

But they were leaving her out of the discussion and that hurt. The link to her past had a strong tug. When her world was a mess, when her life was not her own, those few quiet hours with the shy, fumbling, lost boy had lifted her, she'd felt a kinship with another being, someone as trapped as she.

As much as she trusted Sacha; and she was the one Lyla trusted most of all, experience told her that the Police were an entirely different animal. She had little faith in any 'investigation.' At the back of her mind was the notion that Tom and Sacha had been in a similar situation and had found a way to deal with it. If they could do it, so could she.

Fragments of conversations allied to what had happened in Turkey had taught her enough about Themis to safely assume they had their own way of tidying things up. Sacha had said she'd get a full explanation and that it would be soon but for the moment, she was out of the loop, and patience was not one of her virtues.

This left her mind free to wander its own path, and that path led to a reckoning for Paul Cullen's killer or killers. She had an idea the group would be heading out soon, and if, as she believed, they were following up on Paul, she had no intention of being left out. Paul was part of her story and someone that had got trapped and left behind. She knew she wasn't responsible for any of that, but his sudden death weighed on her in an inexplicable way. When she'd told Sacha she 'owed him', she'd meant it, she had yet to define why.

Deeply nettled, she set aside the things she could nothing about and focussed instead on what she might do. She knew that when everyone was tasked and the estate began to empty, she'd likely be parked with Adey who, from experience, was never far from complete absorption in his work; a window of opportunity would present itself.

As soon as the others left, she'd slip free from Adey and get moving under her own steam. She couldn't take a car, fully acknowledging she wouldn't last five minutes on a public road and getting out of the compound was another problem. She knew she wasn't a prisoner, and that the security systems were there for the benefit of all, but still, she needed to figure out a way of leaving unnoticed. From there she'd hike into the nearest town and bus or train from there.

"Thinking of going somewhere, honey?"

Lyla jerked aware. She'd been lost in the moment and hadn't heard Sacha's approach.

Sacha caught the guilty expression, sat beside Lyla, and turned the laptop screen.

"Paul, huh?"

Lyla nodded mutely, eyes downcast. She was absolutely certain none of the adults understood her point of view and decided to give them one last chance before taking matters into her own hands.

“They gave me to him, like I was nothing, but he didn’t do it, we didn’t do it. Now he’s gone, just gone. It’s not right. I owe him.”

There. She’d said the words that had been smouldering in her mind when looking at his face on the screen. It was a debt. She owed him. It had been a day much like any other. The usual shit. Go here, go there, do this, do that. No will of her own just do as you’re told and no-one, well, you, won’t get hurt. But Paul had flipped the day on its head. Climbing the stairs with him had been repetition, same day, same shit, lie back and think of what Faz’ll do to you if you don’t. But Paul’s refusal, their revolt, the bed bumping had cheated their master’s and felt like a victory for the little guys. Perhaps Paul had mutinied once too often, maybe that’s why she felt like shit, because she hadn’t, ever, well, except just that once and two words now explained what she’d been feeling since seeing the headline. Survivors guilt.

Sacha sat quietly, thinking about the story Lyla had told of two kids who kicked back and shared something. She’d never fully understand Lyla’s life as it had been, but she did appreciate her sadness.

“What would you like to do?”

Lyla looked up; wet eyes loaded with grief.

“I don’t know. Something. Tyrone’s got to be at the bottom of this, he might not have done the stabbing, but if it weren’t for him, Paul would still be alive, would have had a chance to get out.”

Sadly, Sacha recalled the months following Ellens murder, and in remembering, understood the sense of impotence emanating from the girl. Lyla was frustrated by inaction and that meant trouble was brewing. Something had to be done before this turned toxic and Sacha figured she knew just the thing.

"Turn your laptop off and come with me."

"Where to?"

Sacha smiled, remembering back to when she was Lyla's age and her baptism of fire. Her Dad had treated it like a ceremony, preaching safety, respect, and technique. And during it all, Sacha had been absorbed, had felt privileged. Much of her discontent and self-doubt had slipped away with the trust he'd placed in her.

"The bunker."

Lyla's head was spinning, and her right arm ached. The past few hours spent with Sacha had been exhilarating, educational and if it had taught her anything, it was that this group were into self-help in a big way.

Far from taking her mind off events, Lyla was more centred now than she'd ever been. Hasty and half-cocked was not how these people worked and whether they liked it or not, she was going to be one of them. She was going to plan this like a prison escape and knew that bolting from the estate was not the smartest move. From home would be her best option, not from here. Her mind quietened as it began to think logically.

She watched as James and Ollie drove away, guessing correctly that they were heading north. Sacha had said to be ready to leave shortly and was confident that she, Sacha, and Tom would soon be homeward bound.

Lyla waited stoically, quietly adjusting her mind back to when times were hard, when she'd been forced into self-reliance. Ignoring some of the images that resurfaced, she concentrated instead on reassembling her head into survival mode, she'd need it.

The journey home had been uneventful, Lyla communicating as normal, talking dogs, schooling, the stuff of routine. On arrival she'd been left to her own devices and had spent the time fine tuning her plan. Getting to public transport was her first problem. She'd jog it. Whenever they travelled, Tom and Sacha had a mantra. If you can't run with it, don't pack it. Lyla applied the motto by packing only essentials into a backpack.

In her new life, money wasn't a major issue. She earned her allowance by doing what Sacha described as chores and Tom as odd jobs. Helping out in the kennels, walking the dogs, mowing lawns, doing whatever was asked. Sacha and Tom provided her with everything she needed and, having little need to spend, had taken to saving it, describing it auspiciously as her Uni fund.

In deciding to undertake her journey Lyla acknowledged that her running away would hurt Sacha and Tom, in that order. She also knew how tech savvy Themis was and with that firmly in mind, had no intention of switching off her phone or avoiding cashpoints. She wanted to be tracked and found. This was simply a protest, she just needed to get as far away as she could under her own steam, hopefully, in the process, finding Tyrone and then wait until the cavalry arrived. Her point made; she would be included.

WALKABOUT

It was a ritual that neither man acknowledged had developed into a competition. Sid would stroll in, quietly place two identical newspapers on the kitchen table, sit and wait patiently, flicking a biro cap while Tom brewed the coffee. Once the mugs had been set down, the papers would be opened, and unread, flicked to the puzzle section where the crossword waited. No-one kept score but both figured it was about even. Solutions weren't checked, both men had more integrity than that, though occasionally a debate over the veracity or relevance of a particular clue would drive a conversation.

The only modification to this communion would be in high summer, or what passed for it in England. On balmy, sun forecast days, instead of being in the main house first thing in the morning, it would wait until the gardens had been walked, weeded, and tended, coffee would be substituted by cold beer in what had once been the summer house but was now Sid's residence. A status represented by the presence of the Australian Blue Ensign atop Sid's homemade flagpole.

Sid had been with Tom from the beginning, posing as a groundsman and handyman while quietly part of Christian's security team, tasked along with James and Ollie with keeping an eye on Tom. The revelation that Sid wasn't in fact, English, nor in fact either a gardener or a handyman, had at first irked Tom. A temporary attitude as Tom had got to know the man. They were now comfortable with each other, friends, truth be known. It was the gardening that bonded them. The original designer of the house and its grounds had minimalism in mind. Though this term was relative given the size and scope of the plot. Left to its own device's nature would have supplanted ferns with nettles, obscured views and turned pleasant strolls into treks requiring a machete. So, between the two of them, they weeded, planted, maintained, and improved the green areas.

"You Poms don't know how lucky you are."

"How so?"

These debates constantly delighted Tom. Always amused by the Aussie take on the Mother country.

"Well take your stingers for example."

Tom's gloved hand was in the process of tugging a nettle from a border.

"Yeah?"

"Harmless little bugger, that one. For real potency you gotta take a look at a Gympie Gympie." Sid paused for effect.

"It's a bit of a shrub, Queensland way. Touch its leaves or take a lungful of its stinging hairs and you can forget about rational thought for a while, and the pain keeps coming back, for bloody months mate."

"Really." Tom was used to this. He suspected there was a degree of pride attached to the dangers of Australian gardening, most flora and fauna apparently out to get you.

"Oleander will kill you and we plant that as an ornamental."

"Really?"

"Yep. Heart attack, soon as look at ya."

"You don't say."

"Even the Platypus'll have a go. Got spurs on its hind legs. Venomous, mate."

"Right. Then there's the sharks." Ventured Tom.

"Nah." Drawled Sid. "Crocodiles ate all the sharks."

They were halfway through their crossword battle as Sacha came in, fresh from the kennels. Without looking up from his newspaper, Tom spoke.

"She's at it again."

Sacha didn't need to ask. Tom and Inga's long running squabble regarding what he saw as a copse, and Inga regarded as a pet cemetery had been a source of amusement to her since the first fatality had been ceremoniously interred. She figured Tom didn't really mind and was using the situation more for banter than bitching.

"What is it now?"

"Have you been down there? Have you seen it lately?"

Sacha had and had been waiting for this. She walked around the table checking crossword progress like she was looking at hands of cards.

"You're behind." She said, tapping Tom on the shoulder. It was as if a signal had been given.

"Not content with Dream Catchers and mini headstones with faces on, she's added crystals, mirrors, bloody twinkle lights and the wind chimes? Have you heard the row that bamboo, metal, and seashells make? There'll be an altar there any day."

The kitchen door opened, and Inga breezed in, a large boning knife in her hand. Sacha absolutely knew that the implement was purely for Tom's benefit.

"See! Told you. Can't find your cauldron, Inga?"

The breeze outside had taken Inga's habitually untidy hair into another realm. With her free hand she pushed it away from her forehead and gave Tom a glance of feigned distaste.

"Fook off, Tom. It's just feeding time for the boys and girls."

Sacha pulled a large bag of biscuit from her store and calling for Pooh, followed her witchy friend back out to the kennels. Tom smiled, flicked his newspaper with some satisfaction and studied nine across.

"She'll have you one day mate. You see if she doesn't."

Tom glanced up. "You don't believe in all that guff, surely."

Sid grinned. "Can't hurt, mate. What's life without a bit of magic in it?"

Sacha frowned, apparently offended. "What *are* you wearing?"

Tom looked down, stroking the new wool.

"It's a cardigan. Look, it has pockets." He said, proudly.

"You are never, ever going shopping on your own again."

"What? Why?"

Before the questions could be answered, Sid strolled into the kitchen. Tom had just boiled the kettle, looking forward to the crossword tussle then noted with disappointment that the customary newspapers weren't evident.

"She's on her toes. Gone walkabout."

It was morning. They'd been home less than a week before Lyla had done as anticipated.

"Played a blinder," Sid drawled. "I missed it, I spent the night in the kennels. By the way, you have puppies. Out like a rat up a drainpipe she was. Ducked out through the back, the hard way, cross country but keeping to hedgerows, who's been teaching her bushcraft?" Sid shot a knowing look at Sacha, his semi-official role as live-in site security making him more aware than anyone that she and Lyla had been out the past few mornings with the air rifles, rabbiting.

Sacha let it pass and posed a question of her own, one that had worried her from the moment the decision had been made. "How far do we let her get?"

Tom shrugged; he didn't feel particularly involved in this drama and was irritated that his morning routine looked likely to be disrupted.

Sacha gave him a look that spelled trouble then confirmed it by saying pointedly, "Just so you know, Tom. I'm not as relaxed as you about this."

Tom wasn't relaxed, he simply wasn't too disturbed by the current plan to let Lyla off the leash. He was troubled by the youngster's versatility, her talent for blending in. He wondered how much of it was a performance, was she sincere or simply interpreting what she thought was what they wanted. Until he knew, he felt life would be simpler, safer without her. He'd already lost one family and was trying to figure out how to keep its resurrection intact. A reluctant part of him said that didn't include a teenage chameleon, whatever her motives, and he would not, could not, allow her to jeopardise the status quo. He'd yet to work out how to eliminate the worry without anyone getting hurt. So, for now, he'd play the game, stay onside with the woman he adored, for her sake if nothing else. He straightened in his chair and feigned concern.

"Sweetheart. Think back. Remember yourself at that age, and don't try to tell me you never packed a bag just to punish your old man." Tom knew that as a teenager, Sacha had taken juvenile umbrage at some domestic issue with her dad and had dangerously begun to hitch hike across Montana to declare her discontent. It had ended with tears and promises from both sides.

"This is different."

"How?"

Sacha gave her reply some thought. She'd agreed to this rite of passage because she knew that Lyla needed to express some independent thought, and her state of mind under duress tested. The girl had been controlled in one form or another from the age of twelve and she, Tom, and to a lesser degree, Themis knew that they had neither the right nor the inclination to continue the practice.

Paul had been the catalyst, his death had triggered something grim in Lyla, Sacha understood that, she'd been there. With that knowledge Sacha felt strongly that some form of action had been inevitable and however callous this group sanctioned manoeuvre felt, restraining the girl would defeat the object of the exercise. Sacha worried about unforeseen outcomes, had resisted at first but had ultimately accepted that they weren't driving, Lyla was.

Bailey had also sensed the shift in Lyla and had explained that leaving her out of the loop would create resentment and eventually, reaction. The group knew that their security was at risk. They needed to know what form any reaction might take and how it might impact on Themis. Lyla was being tested and at least this way, there'd be oversight, an umbrella. Unknown to her, Lyla's actions had been anticipated and to a point, engineered. Safeguards were in place, tiny electronic tags in clothing and footwear, just in case she tried to avoid detection. Sacha saw the need for it but hated the deception.

"My situation was a world away Tom, I ran away to my grandparents to prove a point, and not a particularly good one. She's not simply running away from something; she's running into something. That makes it different. Edgy"

"Yeah. I know." Tom stood and placed an arm around Sacha's shoulders.

"But I don't fancy jail much and if Themis is to have a future, and if she's going to be part of it, we have to know who or what she is."

"What do you think, Sid?"

Sid had observed this dynamic from a distance and over time, he'd reasoned that Sacha was too involved and Tom too remote. Sid was thoughtful during his hours on the summer house veranda and lately, the difference between nature and nurture had been uppermost in his mind. How that would pan out could only be determined by time, but he knew from her visits and his chats with her, that the girl was just trying to fit in. He'd spent a good deal of time with Lyla since her arrival and as an outwardly disinterested party, felt qualified to comment. Not his usual practice.

"As a rule I keep my oar out but since you pair of throbbers are at odds and you've asked, I reckon she'll be apples. For the record, Sacha, you're too clucky, and you, Tom, need to give her a fair go. Not being judgemental, you understand." With that, he exited the kitchen.

Sacha, mystified, turned to Tom. "Translate, please."

"you're a den mother and I'm an arsehole."

"Apples?"

"He thinks she'll be fine."

"Throbbers?"

"Oh. We're a pair of dickheads."

"Ah. Right."

"I'm surprised she's left her phone on."

"I'm not." Replied Ollie.

Sacha had been in touch; Lyla was on the move. The call itself was unnecessary, James had been tracking her progress up country and reckoned she'd be in town in a few hours and as Sacha would know that, he figured it was just her way of asserting a place in the loop. As far as this experiment was concerned, James leant towards Tom's view. As much as he felt for the kid, the security of the group took precedence. Still, it beat chasing drug dealers for a few days.

"Why's that? She knows we can locate her if she leaves it switched on?"

"Dunno." Replied Ollie, non-committal. "Just a feeling."

Seeing Ollie wasn't going to be drawn, James stretched out on the sofa, hands clasped behind his head. "Whatever."

Lyla knew with some certainty where Tyrone would be. It was term time and schools were where wankers like him would be skulking. She finished her full English, mopping the plate with a slice of bread and lifting her backpack, left the café. This was her third day going solo, shacking up in an Air BnB she'd booked online. Her exit strategy had worked seamlessly. In the early hours, carrying only essentials, she'd crept from the house and avoiding the kennels, which could get noisy, made her way damply across the countryside until the expected main road crossed her line of march. A few miles of trotting and backward glances saw her to civilisation and a bus stop. She'd planned, prepared, and succeeded. It felt good to be doing something and now she was here, where she felt she needed to be, had to be.

It was an odd out of body experience for her, tramping the streets of her hometown. What was once so vilely familiar now had a less threatening air to it. She felt a sense of confidence and freedom that her present anonymity offered. She'd even risked passing by Faz's old fun house, not a pleasant trip down memory lane but it lent her self-imposed mission some hatred to focus on. It was boarded up now, eyeless, and toothless, harmless. She'd even allowed herself a smile on passing the wreck of Badboys Scooby, it was sat on its axles, all the glass had been smashed and the interior stolen. Beneath a bent wiper blade was the remnants of a parking ticket.

Opening her stride, relishing the fit and nourished new identity Sacha and Tom had given her, she rapidly closed the gap between the town and the suburbs, not that suburb was an apt description for the rundown greyness of her old haunts.

It had rained for the first two days and Tyrone had been a no show. The forecast was for a crap but dry day which offered some hope for his making an appearance. Approaching the shithole that was her old seat of learning, she checked the nooks and crannies where she'd spent the past 48 hours of daylight, hopefully unobserved or at least, unremarked. She knew there was a limit to how long she could hang around for and it was fast approaching.

If Tyrone didn't show today, she'd have to beat a temporary retreat and go through a rethink. Her clothing was contemporary and in character, there was nothing about her to attract interest other than that she'd be lurking. The weather helped, cloudy and grey, damp but not wet enough to deter the dealers.

She had limited choices, her patrol area was provincial and vigilant, watchful for the stranger, something she forcefully acknowledged herself to be. Just like yesterday and the day before it, hoping not to be noticed, she opted for another apparently aimless walk by to look for a fresh place to linger. She figured there'd be no one about yet as it wasn't lunchtime or time for the final bell. This was a place where new faces were noticed and she knew that sooner rather than later, she'd be rumbled. Her real problems would start if that 'new face' was recognised as a native. Lyla was desperate to succeed. To get in, find what she needed and get out in one piece and unrecognised. There was more than pride at stake here, but she conceded that it would be pride that would keep her on station longer than was safe. That awareness told her today would probably be her last chance.

The bus stop would be her first post, it was the same sad and natural place to wait.

In another life, she remembered the day it had been installed, shiny and brand new, but not for long. Nothing new survived around here, all it could do was endure and being static, it became an immediate target. No glass in it; there hadn't been for years, and the Perspex replacement, once pristine and transparent had been scraped, scratched, chipped and a target for graffiti. But battered and decaying, it blended in with its surroundings and was therefore unremarkable, it would do for the twenty minutes she needed.

There was no timetable to read, having been stolen for no singular purpose within minutes of installation but had there been, she'd have taken no time studying it, locals didn't do that. Instead, she reached into her hoodie pocket and took out the bog standard, state of the ark, pay as you go she'd picked up from the newsagents earlier. She kept her new iPhone nestled in her rucksack, away from prying, acquisitive eyes, hidden but passively declaring her whereabouts. She puzzled briefly why no-one had come for her yet, not even a phone call or text. Had she pushed them too far by absconding? For a split second her faith in them wavered. Then, thinking of Paul, she gathered her resolve and clenched her teeth, knowing she couldn't chicken out now, there would be no crawling back, if she was on her own, well, it wouldn't be the first time. She began scrolling, turbo thumbed, doing what teenagers do, except she wasn't. She was watching.

"She alright?"

"As far as I can tell. Can't see much from here."

James and Ollie were stationed nearby. Line of sight but not much else. Like Lyla, they too, were watching, they had Lyla's back.

She'd moved from the bus stop to the chip shop, she knew that provided you got your timing right, the takeaway had the gravitational pull of a small planet to kids and as a consequence, the dealers.

She was hunched over a polystyrene box chewing unenthusiastically on greasy chips she neither needed nor wanted when at last, Tyrone showed up. Though his kingdom had moved from the classroom to the street, the bullying swagger was still evident. Blinged up, he cuffed his way to the front of the queue. She noted that no money went over the counter in exchange for the food. Remembering Badboy had a relationship with a takeaway she looked hard at the proprietor. Seeing nothing but resentment settled her, established that the relationship was one sided and likely based on fear, but not of Tyrone who had yet to become a full-grown adult. It wasn't news to her that Ty was part of something bigger, that was how it worked around here. Lyla noted that despite now being a street dealer, Tyrone had yet to graduate from stealing dinner money and pulling hair. She'd watched as he'd grabbed the occasional kid, unnecessarily delivering a slap or a kick. She felt a ripple of anger and suffocated it. There was nothing she could do but stay out of sight and watch. She needed to find out where he went after his drops or pickups and she was wary, these were not friendly streets.

With meat on her bones and an assured carriage, she felt and looked unrecognisable, not a grain of the half-starved stray dog she'd once been remained. But there was always a chance encounter that could expose her. She had no idea what had been happening here or who was still about. She picked up the vibe of a nervous tingle on the back of her neck, and something told her it was time to go. That was when she felt the hand on her shoulder.

There was a whisper in her ear. "Boo."

She turned and instinctively lashed out, feet kicking, hands scratching towards the voice. Then there was another body behind her, blocking her escape. The two pressed together, penning her in, gripping her wrists.

"Lyla! The tone wasn't threatening, more cautionary.

She looked up from her blind funk and in grateful recognition, stopped struggling. They hadn't forgotten her.

"Ollie! You fucking twat!"

As one rarely went anywhere without the other, she guessed that James was to her rear. Her notion was confirmed when she heard him speak.

"I told you not to sneak up on her from behind. She's a trained killer, anything could have happened."

Ollie grinned, nursing his scraped shins. "Come on kids, let's away."

Libby could not believe her eyes. No-one took a blind bit of notice when she'd tried to tell them about the hot basement and the fat policeman, gunshots and girls not coming back. Fucking SAS rescuing damsels in distress was all bollocks, they'd scoffed. They thought the squaddies, swimming pool, the villa, the sunshine was a complete fantasy, that she'd been in rehab or spaced out, not on a jolly.

It didn't help that she'd been drugged for the journey home and had no memory of it, simply a jerk from one reality, the villa, to another, the fucking rehab shithole. But faces, she was good with faces. And right now, she was looking straight at three she'd never forget. And every one of them had been at that fucking villa. When she'd tried to tell it, the only part of her tale that had resonated with Tyrone was the name of the posh bitch, Lyla. He'd laughed at that, at the idea that Lyla would ever be anything other than what she was, a scutter from the gutter. He'd told her to fuck off, that she'd just thrown in a name everybody on the circuit had known, but who had disappeared, and therefore couldn't be grilled. Libby was a lot of things and that was her problem. She'd lied before and would again but for once she had proof; it was large as life and standing outside the chippy.

Libby smiled as she tried to figure out a way of isolating the bitch from the two minders. That weird shit that had happened was the only thing that made her interesting, and Libby desperately wanted to be different from the others, to Ty at least, especially now Faz was gone.

Nothing came to mind, so she opted to leave the thinking to Ty. He'd know what to do. Her story would be listened to rather than mocked and with a bit of luck there might be some free gear coming her way with the telling and retelling of it. With that thought Libby turned away and quickened her step to Tyrones gaff.

"So, it was a test?" The drive back had been informative.

"Sort of." Replied James. "There were just a few things we had to know."

"Such as?" Lyla wasn't happy, but sort of was. She wasn't happy now she knew her escape had been anticipated, that her intention had been so transparent, but was relieved that they'd been there for her. What the test was she had no idea and she'd been promised a full explanation on arrival back at the big house. They were nearly there.

"What things?"

"Can't say." Said Ollie. "Goes against the creed."

"Your Mom'll tell you." James offered, knowing that the use of the matronymic would please the girl. And it did.

The gates opened and further up the driveway past the bunker, Lyla could see Sacha and Tom waiting by the house. The car had barely halted as Lyla leapt from it and rushed towards them. She reached Sacha first and was enveloped, wanting more, her head burrowed into Sacha's body, and she reached out with her arm, creating a space which in a moment or two, Tom filled. The three of them stood there momentarily until Sacha disengaged, holding Lyla at arm's length.

"Am I in trouble?"

Tom smiled and it seemed that in that moment some doubt in his expression was swept away. Lyla sensed it more than saw it. "Not as much as you should be."

Sacha pulled her in again. "You're grounded."

Tyrone was in deep shit. He'd turned the place upside down and there was no sign of it. He'd hidden it under his mattress. He absolutely knew he had and now it was gone. He sat on the edge of his bed, his head in his hands. He'd have to get out. He'd take the stash he had and with no idea where to go, he'd leave. The kid that called himself Snake had warned him.

"It's a one off. Just for this job. The man wants it back."

He'd done exactly what he was told. Sent the fat twat off on a train knowing he wouldn't be coming back. The phone had been a crucial part of that, untraceable, expensive, as irreplaceable as he was expendable.

As soon as he'd got the nod that the kid was done, he'd followed the instructions to the letter. Switched the phone off and hidden it until someone came to pick it up. But it was gone and no amount of looking was going to change that.

He looked around his room. Downstairs he could hear his Mum 'n 'Stepdad' arguing, stuff being thrown around, the usual bollocks. Them he wouldn't miss but just as he was getting somewhere, this had to happen. He wouldn't be believed, there'd probably be torture, murder, his mind worked frantically through all the excuses, the promises he might try to make but he knew it wouldn't do him one little bit of good.

Kids like him disappeared all the time, runaways, probably gone to London. But some never got that far and if he stayed here he knew he'd be one of them, like Cullen. His past misdemeanours would catch up with him in the papers. Not that he'd get to read them. Truant, probably into drugs, troublesome, uncooperative, his grim school reports as much as an epitaph as he'd likely receive. Tyrone wanted to weep, knowing what was coming and uncertain as to how to avoid it.

The only glimmer of light, and he was trying to work his head around it, was the apparent reappearance of the skinny bitch, Lyla. Only not skinny now, posh, fed and Gucci'd up.

Like everybody, Ty had heard the rumours, the gossip, firmed up by the paedo ring going awol and the house shutting down. Lyla was the only link and he hated that he only vaguely remembered her, only that she'd been a pony him and his mates used to ride.

Libby had been babbling on for months about some weird shit that had gone down. Sunshine villa and a free holiday, but Libby was a junkie and most of the shite that came out of her mouth was bollocks. But this new snippet of info about Lyla and her two minders had Tyrone's imagination going. He struggled with the idea that all along, despite her previous form, Libby might have been telling the truth, she wasn't known for it. But what if she was?

Nah. No way. Ok, so what if it was all complete shite, if he could get her to be convincing enough, he might yet get off the hook. A story formed that if he could believe enough in it himself, he'd be able to persuade others of it. The phone wasn't lost. He'd been ripped off. No, he didn't know why but he figured that the drugs ring was the target, he was just a victim. Somewhere out there was something that was coming for them and if the trash talk was straight, a very organised something as it had already knocked off Faz 'n his mates, and fucked up some local dealers, who was to say they hadn't set their sights on Ty?

He'd sort Libby, she needed to get her story straight, make it believable, fuck off all the shit about guns and rescues, just make it about the competition. That would do it. Someone was trying to take over.

PLAN A

Lyla was allowed to sit in and was basking in acceptance. Sacha had explained that this was to be a slow process and argued correctly that some knowledge of the background of the group does not mean unrestricted access to operations but for this phase, she was to be included.

In the few days she'd been away, she learned that James and Ollie, working with all of Themis's resources, had identified, followed, and burgled Tyrone. It was, she'd been told in no uncertain terms, a lesson in teamwork. If she was to be part of this, she needed to share, to conform. It was a lesson she took to heart.

James and Ollie took coffee from the counter and joined the others at the conference table. Bailey stood and walked the short distance to her whiteboard and projector screen. In her hand, she held the results of James and Ollie's breaking and entering.

"This," She began, lifting the phone, "Is a little beauty. I downloaded and translated the contents. Electronically, I hasten to add, a lot of it is in Albanian which isn't on my CV. It's interesting reading." She handed out printed A4 sheets.

"Albanian?" Interrupted Ames. This was the first suggestion that there was a new group involved. "In charge or just doing the donkey work?"

"Sorry, Boss. There's a new kid in town. It's across the board. At the top of the tree, is a family, of sorts, ethnic by nature. Linked to a single individual, Altin Cela by name. You'd think their persec would be better."

"What's persec?"

"Personal security, honey," Sacha replied. "Now hush." Lyla fell silent, trying to process.

Bailey continued. "This phone and the technology it contains is an indicator that they're serious players. These do not grow on trees and there's a reason for that and for their slack persec." She nodded towards Lyla, putting the word into context for her. She glowed at the inclusion.

"They assumed they were OK. This phone has Encrochat installed, and for added security, GPS, microphones, and cameras removed. It's a Dutch system with ultramodern encryption, completely legal but its sole purpose is to frustrate the collection of evidence or intelligence. Thieving it prevented the hitting of the panic wipe button, a sexy feature that does what it says on the tin. It took four years of work for the French and Dutch authorities to crack the system and they've been quietly stalking the platform for a while now.

Think Bletchley and Enigma. Like the Nazi's, the crooks have no idea their every word, written or spoken, is being monitored and have no idea what's coming. Worldwide, criminal networks are about to be busted wide open."

"And you've been able to access that in the same way?"

"That's what I do." Bailey stated, simply.

Quizzical expressions demanded further explanation. Bailey made it small.

"Shared intel is vulnerable. I just accessed the joint Dutch/French database." No-one asked how and Bailey didn't elaborate.

James was thoughtful, then spoke. "So even if a phone gets lost, mislaid or stolen, our European friends' activities aside, they'll be confident it can't be hacked?"

"Completely." Replied Bailey. "Phones can get lost, stolen, no matter how careful they are. And of course, because of the built in or removed security systems, they have no idea where they are or who has them. But they'll be confident the batteries will eventually die, and likely carry on as normal. Anything else you need clarifying?" It sounded like a rebuke but wasn't, it was simply Bailey's way of working efficiently.

"Lesson over. Now to business. Our lead guy, Altin Cela." She touched a button on a small remote control. The wall screen filled with moving images showing the inside of a commercial gym, a tall, saturnine, muscled figure drawing water from a free-standing cooler.

"Or at least that's who he purports to be, there's really no way of knowing his true background. Came across illegally, paperless, stateless, claimed asylum, spoke to the right people, did all the right things and now, some five years on, is for all intents and purposes, an immigrant success story. And you'll never guess which lawyer eased his entry."

Uniquely, PC had asked to sit in on the briefing and was at the back of the room next to Lyla. He shifted uncomfortably in his chair, clearly troubled with guilt by association. There was only one legal giant common to all.

"Owns a string of gyms and night clubs. Outwardly a self-made man. But the contents of the phone you took tell a completely different and altogether more noxious tale. Albanian, as mentioned and a well-connected criminal one. As you'd expect, there's not much he's not in to. Drugs, guns, people trafficking, prostitution."

Ames interrupted apologetically, indicating the moving images on the screen.

"When was that taken?"

"It's live."

"Really?

"Oh yes. Really. On the surface, our boy is a model citizen. That includes installing CCTV in all his 'legitimate' businesses. Naturally, they're run from computers and in virtually all cases, if those computers are connected to the net as most are, remotely accessible."

Bailey shrugged; no more words were needed. Then continued.

"But this is where it gets interesting, and I'll try and keep this brief. Cocaine is a South American export with Columbia as a main source. The problem with Columbia from the smugglers point of view is that the government, with the help of the DEA, is making life difficult. A crackdown on corruption and massively increased security at points of exit, ports, airports, and the like has pushed the cartels to look elsewhere for export opportunities. Southwards in this case where Columbia shares a porous border with Ecuador, much of which is criss-crossed with tangled, jungle waterways which a small boat can easily navigate. Most of it is transported to and shifted from Guayaquil, Ecuador's main city and port on the west coast. From there it goes one of two ways, the Pacific route for our American friends and the Amazon route, through the Panama Canal, docking at Rotterdam or Antwerp in contaminated cargo shipping for the

European market. To give you an idea of the scale of the problem facing the authorities there, the port of Rotterdam is 42km long and processes 23,000 containers daily. Their most recent drugs seizure, 8000kg, was found in a container of bananas and had a street value of almost 600 million euros. Similarly, Antwerp manages in excess of 20,000 containers daily. You can imagine the rest. As far as we're concerned, there are references on here to Paul, Tyrone and another player, Leon by name. His murder was pre-planned, it doesn't say why. Sorry Lyla."

Lyla kept her head up, determined that this was business and that she would be seen to be treating it as such.

"Ok." Said James. "And this interests us how? We're not a government agency. This is way beyond our brief. In that phone is everything we need to know about Lyla's friend and what happened. Our job's done, isn't it time we handed over what we know?"

Ames stepped in. He'd been waiting for an opportunity such as this and the one presenting itself was exactly the kind of operation the group needed. A quick in and out, now you see me, now you don't, with a concrete result. It would get the group focussed and nicely oiled for anything larger that might come up.

"You're right, we have what we needed, and justice could be served. But that phone is a gold mine, and we can't ignore the possibilities it presents."

"Yeah, I get that, but what's all this about Ecuador, Rotterdam, Antwerp?"

"Well," replied Ames. "We think we should give him a bigger problem to worry about than a lost phone."

"Meaning?"

Bailey held up the burgled phone. "He has a large consignment arriving imminently. It's comparable in size and value to the massive one seized in Rotterdam." She looked at Ames who finished the sentence.

"We're going to steal it."

Showered, Altin mentally shelved what for now was a minor inconvenience. The loss of an Encrochat phone he would worry about later, there was also the issue of the person that had lost it. His immediate concern was a container arriving from Rotterdam and the bulk shipment hidden within. He had no doubt it would clear on arrival in Holland and again when it unloaded in Grimsby.

The method and route had been tested, the right palms greased or coerced. Until now, he had relied upon shipments coming in piecemeal. This was the big one, the expansion his brother had said should be low and slow. But Bujar wasn't here, and Altin had a free hand. One he intended to exercise. Everything, his present and future, depended on it going smoothly, then he could show his brother just how powerful and organised he had become, how he had surpassed even Bujar's vision of the Cela legacy.

DYNO ROD

"Right then What's the plan? What do we do with the drugs once we've got them?"

Ames looked up from behind his desk.

"It seems to me Ollie, that simply stealing them would create enough of a problem for our boy. 500 million sterling isn't to be sniffed at."

"Saw what you did there, Boss, nice one. But you're not thinking this through."

Ames sat across from Ollie who, Ames noted curiously, even ominously, had Adey, their resident chemist, in tow. These two were not natural bedfellows, he would need to be wary.

"My intention was to anonymously get it to the authorities for destruction. You have another idea?"

Ollie leaned forwards; his fingers knitted together. "Just nicking the stuff won't finish it. We need to seriously fuck him up. The drugs can be replaced, so the cycle continues, life goes on. Reputations though, well, they take some making and once lost…"

Ames conceded the point. In a world where criminal activity is salient, prestige and stature led to a perverse eminence. "Go on."

"Some years back, I used to play squash with a guy. He rarely won which I guess, with hindsight, ticked him off a bit."

Ames couldn't see where this was going but while listening, from the corner of his eye was watching Adey nod enthusiastically, his eyes alive, eager to join the conversation.

"Anyway, one day, after a game in which he was particularly humiliated, he offered me a piece of gum, chewing gum. Very sporting, I thought, taking it, and popping it in my mouth." Ollie paused for effect.

"I spent the next 24 hours on the shitter emptying my guts out. It was horrific, be glad this story 'aint scratch 'n sniff."

Ames recoiled mentally at the proffered image. "It was a laxative?"

"Indeed, it was, and a particularly effective one at that. Took me years and a friendly chemist to get that wanker back."

Chemist, there was that word again, and he had one in the room.

"And your point? Forgive me for stating what I believe is the obvious, but you must ingest a laxative for it to actually have an effect. I'm not sure snorting Ex-Lax will do the trick."

Ollie leant back in his chair, folding his arms, and conceding the floor. “Adey, tell the man.”

“NDDS.” It had been a long time since Adey had been given an opportunity to talk science. Given its intended use, even Ollie had listened. He wasn’t about to let this opportunity slip away.

“What?”

“Nano Drug Delivery System.” Adey launched into the description proper.

“The pharmacokinetics and pharmacodynamics of a drug are highly dependent on its physical and chemical features, and it’s influenced by the type of formulation used to deliver it. By scaling down the size of the compounds, nano-DDS can modulate and improve the performance of many drugs to an extent not achievable by conventional formulations. We can taint the cocaine.”

Ames shook his head, not to indicate negativity but to clear it, the science had escaped him on the uttering of the word pharmacokinetics.

“Everything you’ve just said went over my head. But are you saying you can deliver a laxative nasally?”

“Well,” replied Adey, “Theoretically yes, though it’s never been tested.”

“I should bloody well hope not.” Retorted Ames. Horrified, yet interested. He could instantly see some virtue in the idea.

“There’s more.” Said Ollie. Grinning from ear to ear.

“Oh, I can’t wait.” Was all Ames could manage.

“That presentation earlier, in the Gym, there was a water cooler.” Ollie reminisced.

“So?”

Adey leant forward, enjoying the conspiracy and the audience.

“A water-soluble compound. Most compounds can be crystallised. Think about boiling salt water and seeing a crust on the pan. It comes down to the rate of evaporation, the rate of heating, cooling etc.”

Ames held up a hand. “Stop. Wait. Give me a minute.”

“Boss.” Asserted Ollie, sensing that Ames might be warming to the idea. “Think about it. Whatever the science, and I don’t get it either but apparently, we can spike the coke, and as an extra bonus we can sabotage the coolers in every gym he owns. Not only do we destroy his drugs, but we also destroy his reputation, his businesses. Imagine, a brown Tsunami laid at this fucker’s door. He’ll never, ever live it down.”

In the quiet that followed, Ames focussed on the 'brown tsunami' element of the proposal. There might be a lesson here for everyone, users, and suppliers.

"How long?"

"How long what?"

"How long do you need to make the compound you've just described?"

"Well," Replied Adey. "If the 500 million figure is accurate, I'd estimate that to be about 8,000 kilograms of base product. With some help, I could knock up enough Dyno Rod overnight to treat that. The water is easy, He's got 5 Gyms, two coolers in each. 10 carboys of pre-treated H2O won't take long at all."

"Dyno Rod?"

"Well, I'm not planning on patenting it, so I just borrowed a name to suit the process."

The idea appealed to Ames. Capture and prosecution were accepted by criminals as an occupational hazard and could even be seen as kudos. Humiliation on the other hand…was career ending. Ames really didn't like the look of this Altin character. He knew the type, had seen this smugness and conceit countless times across the table in an interview room. It had maddened him then, it maddened him now. But this time, he wasn't shackled by rules. Reputation was everything to the career criminal and Ames liked the idea of buffing off some of the perverse gloss career criminals seemed to attain. The more he extrapolated, the more appealing some of the possible side effects of the proposed course of action took root in his mind. Scatological references, every know pun regarding shit would be forever associated with Mister Cela. The schoolboy in him smiled.

"Off you pop. Borrow anyone who isn't busy." Said Ames, several further possibilities presenting themselves. "Dave and Neil are on task as we speak, hopefully the drugs will be here sometime in the next few days."

Mulling over what the effects of Adey's contribution might be, Ames wandered into Bailey's office, briefed her on the proposed modification, then sat, watching her think.

"So?"

"It's a unique proposal, I'll grant them that."

"Can it be done, logistically?"

"Well giving the drugs back rather than having them destroyed does make it a bit trickier but I can manage the paper and electronic trail." Bailey replied. "Computers may make admin simpler, but it also means theft is a snip."

"So, where are we?" Asked Ames.

“Well, we know the route, container, and bill of lading number thanks to the boys’ skills at larceny and the crook’s utter reliance on the Encrochat system. I’m tracking the ship live using its own Automatic Identification System, or AIS number. Each container has a unique tracking device, or CTD. I have access to that data. I’m just in the process of switching its ID to another, innocent container so we can drive it out of the docks. The fly in the ointment with this fresh idea is that our physical presence at the docks goes beyond a simple theft, we need to do a substitution. Getting the stuff back into place after treatment won’t be easy.”

Bailey, frowned, thinking, then appeared to win some internal battle. “As far as the notification system goes, I’ll feed in a 48-hour delay to the Albanian, engine trouble at sea affecting the cargoes ETA. That’ll give the guys an overnight window to do the deed and us time to mess up the product and get it back. Once they’ve dropped back off, I’ll throw a virus into the dock computer system, just because I can. After that, it’s in the lap of the gods but even if we can’t get it back in place, at least the dealers won’t have it.”

Ames had considered that when debating the idea himself. Either way, it was win, win.

“I’ll let them know the plan has changed.”

It was 10pm and Immingham was still 2 hours away. Neil and Dave with their minds on the arrivals process. With what they now knew, it was fairly obvious why Immingham had been selected as the port of entry. A lot could go unseen or adrift in the mass that was, by tonnage, far and away the largest port in the UK. They were en route to add some subterfuge to the chaos.

"How did you get into motors in such a big way?"

The motorway was monotonous, the silence in the truck enlivened only by Neil swearing at dickheads.

"Mm? Oh. I started young I guess, got to drive loads of different cars 'n stuff. Some proper fancy ones."

"Car thief?"

"Fuck off, Dave. My Dad had a car delivery service, I used to move stuff all over the country then hitch-hike home. Some of 'em occasionally broke down; I had to develop skills or get pissed wet through waiting for recovery."

"That's it?"

"Sorry. Yep. Boring. If you can't fix it with a hammer, you've got an electrical problem. What about you?"

"Same thing I s'pose. Stuff that's supposed to be squaddie proof snaps in half or doesn't work properly in the first place. I got tired of waiting for the armourers to finish their tea breaks. Learnt how to do it myself."

"That doesn't explain where you get 'stuff' from."

Neil had seen inside Dave's workshop. There were racks of assorted weaponry and exotic, shiny bits of military kit even the British Army didn't have. He was curious to know where it all came from and how Dave imported it.

"You know how it is, mate. Contacts."

Neil racked his brains for names, desperate to hit back at the 'car thief' arrow Dave had fired off.

"Adnan Khashoggi? Viktor Bout?" Both were well known and notorious names in the arms trade, unfortunately for Neil, his recollections were unreliable.

"One's dead, the other one's in jail. And if you work my side of the track, the last thing you want to be is a registered firearms dealer."

"So, you thought about that?"

"Not really, legit imports into the UK aint lethal enough but you know how it is. It was more of a happy accident than a career choice. Mates pick up souvenirs, smuggle stuff back from overseas contracts. Have you got any idea how much stuff was dumped overboard from the Canberra when the Paras came back from the

Falklands? Word got around kit was gonna be searched for booty. Plymouth Sound is full of gear that made a splash. No good now though. Be well rusty." He added gloomily, "but you get the picture."

Neil did, having heard the stories, but that didn't explain where Dave got all the modern equipment he had access to. He decided that as no explanation was forthcoming, he'd make something up, to pass the time.

"Didn't I read somewhere that an armoury was broken into?"

"Just concentrate on the road, Neil. But that's why I always have a false passport handy." The motorway became monotonous again.

On the horizon, announcing its presence from miles away, Immingham glowed like a bushfire. Following ample signage in a variety of languages, Neil pulled the container truck up to reception, showed his documents and the bored staffer on minimum wage waved them through with the vague location of their load.

Though it was 2am, the place was lit as if it were daylight. But there were shadows cast by the sodium arc lights and it was in that merger of gloom and the protection of the truck's bulk that they would get the job done. The combination of a physical description and the CTD locator led them to their target, innocent in appearance amongst thousands of siblings, but sitting there like a modern-day Pandora's Box. Neil thumbed a button on the small device Bailey had issued him, waving it around, as if it made a difference. It sent a signal to the CTD, frazzling its circuits, at the same time, taking out some blameless units nearby.

Beside him, Dave checked the locator, nodding as the signal died. On instructions from Bailey, Dave had prepared a 'wrap.' A vinyl, adhesive sheet printed upon which were the details of their wholly innocent unit. Taking spray bottles and squeegees they overlaid the markings and loaded up. That done, they wandered around frying random CTD locators, making future identification of anything on site a manual, laborious process. Satisfied sufficient mayhem had been caused to the collection process, they exited the docks, it had taken twenty minutes. Within 24 hours, it was back, the wrap disguise removed, its contents no longer as pure as Altin liked to boast.

LOST AND FOUND

Vehicular access had been restricted to those contractors who could physically identify their loads. Outside the gates, and on the roads that led to them, queues of trucks added to the anarchy that had descended on what was usually a calm and efficient process. Local cafes were brimming with grumpy truckers and tempers were beginning to fray. There was a larger than usual police presence, tired drivers and tight manoeuvring causing the occasional collision, drivers frequently coming to blows. Local traffic management was slipping out of hand as side roads filled with new arrivals simply trying to find somewhere to lay up until the mess got sorted. Offshore anchorages were full, and the unloading of ships that had managed to dock had been temporarily halted, the site now crammed with uncollected containers. This at least meant that in an effort to clear the backlog, contractors were permitted to look for their loads on foot. Among the confusion, a disbelieving but relieved Kreshnik double checked the paperwork in his hand and glanced again at the markings on the container. They matched. He crossed himself in gratitude. Computers had failed, he'd been told, if you absolutely can't wait, try and find it yourself. Something he'd been increasingly desperately attempting to do since arriving, a process hampered by other, equally frustrated but at least legitimate haulage contractors. He was absolutely certain he'd checked this very area only yesterday. Perhaps in his haste, it had been overlooked, the letters and numbers blurring under scrutiny. Containers went missing all the time, locators fail, they'd had a bunch go dead a few nights ago; probably an atmospheric spike, the administrator bluffed, darkly aware that as importers go, the man had little interest in bananas.

Paperwork goes adrift they'd told him; the containers usually turn up. Kreshnik didn't share the relaxed attitude of the Dock management. Banana's spoil, he'd told them, in an effort to speed things up. He looked again at the rear of the container and back to his paperwork. Then picked up his phone.

"Say that again, slowly."

"I've found it, boss. The seals are intact. I'm getting it to the warehouse now."

Kreshnik waited, relations between he and Altin had been frayed these past two days. He liked his job and wanted to keep it; he held his life in even higher regard and though no direct threats had materialised, he knew by Altins tone that the situation was not to his pleasing.

In 48 hours, he'd gone from being a person responsible for the collection, to being *the* person responsible for its loss. The injustice of it was purely academic. Someone always paid for failure;

and termination usually meant something more permanent than simple unemployment in his line of work. Finding the container was a life saver, in many ways. The system failure at Immingham was national news but Altin wasn't interested how or why his unit wasn't where it should be, which was safely tucked away in his warehouse. Kreshnik rubbed at tired eyes, directed the loading of the container then followed the temporary one-way system, out of what had become his own, personal hell. It didn't matter what had happened, it was here now, and in one piece, there was no need to tell the Boss he'd overlooked the unit during his earlier search.

In his office, Altin worked his way through a variety of emotions and anxieties. Relief that the cocaine had finally been found, frustration at the delay, anger that one of the wheels; the most important wheel of his operation had almost fallen off. This was his biggest shipment to date, enough to supply this shithole of a country for months. But his 8 tonnes were now en route and would shortly be unloaded, split, packaged then lost in the system.

He knew his market, the UK consumes around 30 tonnes a year, or 10 billion pounds worth. That shipment would net him around 30% of the trade, a share he'd intended to grow. He'd spent the last five years of his life building up a network, violently closing rivals down, absorbing others just for this moment. Had it been lost, the financial hit meant that there would be no hiding from his brother, family or not.

The temporary loss of the container had worn him thin, the finding of it, the beginning of a new era. His Kryetar's had their systems and people in place. The underbosses would see to the larger consignments going out by road, the smaller markets, one's he hoped to grow, were tended by his County Lines mules.

He anticipated some small losses but in the great scheme of things, the cash would be rolling in by midweek, the partygoers fully stocked up by the weekend with enough spare coke, his coke, rolling around in the system to keep them happy for months. Life was good. The question of the lost phone had yet to be addressed. He'd give it his full attention next week. He bit on an apple and as he chewed, studied the perfect toothmarks in the fruit.

BUDDY'S

Ginge and Kim were at their usual post, usual that is for this time on a Friday. Buddy's, their nightclub, had yet to hit the magic hour, that time of the evening when downstairs got so busy the door had to start knocking back the unknown or unruly. So, they spent the first few hours in the calmness of the entrance, watching the familiar street, getting a feel for the mood of the town.

No local football this weekend; nice, less chance of any madness kicking off but being the last weeks of summer, you could never tell, and it was always worth sniffing the air. They'd had the club for some years now and Buddy's was part of the fabric of the town. This small part of Leicestershire was fond of its fixtures and they of it.

Few folks recalled the time when the reason for Ginge's nickname was at once, visually plain. His scalp had been smooth for years, but the nickname remained. A dark, well fitted suit buttoned tight over a stomach too fond of ale but middle aged now, he wasn't that stressed by it and Kimmy didn't seem to mind.

Kim stood beside him, smiling and chatting to the sparse, early evening crowd. Streaked, blonde/ash shoulder length hair framing a generous expression, she wore a bluish green silk blouse and dark leather trousers, finishing off with something comfortable for the feet. The hours were long but, Ginge mused, better than driving a truck for a living.

Inside, the club was starting to fill so Mitch climbed the stairs up to street level, gratefully leaving the beat behind and nodding to Ginge and Kim that it was now his watch. This was the routine, time for the owners to mingle with the punters. They relinquished their posts and headed down into the lights, lasers, and fog.

Mitch was troubled, not to the point of bothered but troubled, nevertheless. He'd had burnt pizza for supper last night. Not from choice, but his domestic arrangements of late had been less than ideal. At weekends he rarely got home before 3 or 3.30 am, there was the kicking out to do, check the premises, have a quick drink with the staff and then head home. There'd been a time when she'd stay up and wait, warm a supper for him and chat about the evening's events, but those days appeared to be a thing of the past.

Lately he'd returned to a darkened flat, starving, and weary with the aura of burning martyr emanating from the bedroom, he'd taken to keeping a stash of frozen pizzas and throwing one in the oven. But too often he'd doze off as it cooked, then blackened, then smoked. His girlfriend was kicking back, hating the hours he did, insisting he quit, or she'd do one.

He didn't do this for the money. He did it because he genuinely enjoyed it and figured there was no-one else did it better. Mitch was old school and an unlikely looking Head Doorman. 5'9" and 14 stone he'd often been underestimated by the uneducated or unwary. Mitch knew, and they'd learnt, it wasn't the dog in the fight that mattered, it was the fight in the dog. Mitch ran a tight ship, and everyone knew it.

The players: and he knew exactly who they were, if they came to his club, were under no illusions that there was to be no dealing, if they came, it was to spend, not earn, so they tended to stay away, finding easier pickings elsewhere.

There were the inevitable pills that changed hands inside and there was little to be done about that, the transactions too small and easily hidden, so he tolerated it unless they were blatantly taking the piss. But the coke was a different matter. It couldn't all be prevented, the body searches were for knives, the bag searches for booze, but his door was as clean as it could get. The club's reputation for cleanliness however, along with virtually every other late night entertainment venue this side of the border, was about to take a hit.

Most folk do their drugs before hitting a venue, the chances of getting kicked out if caught doing it al fresco being too high. So, in the privacy of their own homes while priming the night out with a cheap booze of choice, they lay the lines down and got ready to hit the town. Once oiled up though, and in the babel of a busy night club, some caution is set aside, top up hits taken swiftly off the hand or bombed. The bomb was preferable if trying to avoid detection and is a quantity of coke wrapped in a rizla and swallowed. Not only had you got your hit, but there was also no external evidence that you'd actually had it.

But this was where Adey's delivery method took a different and entirely unexpected turn. 'Bombing', hadn't been considered when contaminating the product and once gastric acid ate away at the fag paper, the cocaine, and anything in it, was released directly into the stomach. Worse still, any user with a grain of self-respect knows that for the coke to take effect in a bomb, you need to ingest a larger quantity of the product and whatever might be in it, the downside of this to the user is that it's wasteful and its effects take longer to be felt. But not tonight, at least not in the case of the Dyno Rod additive.

The coke snorted before arrival was quietly going about its business, as predicted slowly releasing the drug into the bloodstream, and making its way to the pleasure centres of the brain. Meanwhile, Adey's NDDS additive was on an altogether more disturbing mission, slowly working its way via the bloodstream into the gut, where it was gently working its magic. But the abrupt introduction of a neat dose of Dyno Rod to the 'bombers' stomachs had a creeping but ultimately explosive effect. Adey had opted for a stimulant laxative, fast acting, it animates the nerves in the colon and the rectum which causes the muscles of the large bowel to squeeze harder than usual. This pushes the faeces along and out, spectacularly, as it happened. The party began with an unusual abundance of flatulence, creating much merriment and a good deal of showing off among most of the gentlemen and some of the ladies. Few things are as funny as a fart, until it isn't. Ask the girl who attempted one in a jacuzzi full of her friends.

The message in his earphone was the first Mitch knew was that there was a disturbance in the toilets. This was a regular occurrence, the *who are you looking at?* crowd generally took their grievances there. He shouldered his way down the stairs and around the outside edge of the dance floor but was stopped by Ginge, who, generally cheerful and unflappable, was anything but.

"I wouldn't go in there if I were you."

"For fuck's sake, Ginge, move out of the way. We need to stop this."

Ginge raised his eyebrows. "Really?" His accent distinctly local, the word came out as 'Realleh?' more as an idiom than the single word usually signified, expressing disbelief rather than a query.

Ginge stepped aside, clearing Mitch's route. "Be my guest but unless you've got a pocketful of corks, I don't reckon you can, mate. Can't you smell it?"

Kimmy, right behind him, was wide eyed and similarly distracted. She glanced back over her shoulder in horror at what appeared to be a growing crisis. "Jesus fucking Christ, Mitch. It's carnage."

Mitch was at a loss. Fights were meat and drink to him and easily defused or resolved. This was obviously not one of those situations. "What the fuck is actually happening back there?"

Kim arched a delicate, precise eyebrow. "It's a shit storm, Mitch and I mean literally a shit storm. We're closing."

Mitch opened his mouth then shut it again. *Closing?* He watched as Ginge muscled his way to the DJ's booth.

The aroma and cries of distress and conflict reached Mitch simultaneously. There were two unusually active crowds between him and the toilets, one desperately trying to get in, the other frantic to get away. But it was his door, and as much as the odour he was headed towards became more striking and the rush for the exits more appealing, he knew he had to get a firsthand look at what exactly was going on.

Behind him he vaguely heard Ginge shout at the DJ. In response, the music shut down and the guru on the turntables began issuing surprise instructions to leave, that the club was closing for the night.

The main lights came on and Mitch got a clearer view of the melee as he was jostled on all sides. Deciding to deal with what he knew best, he took the gents first, a sleeve over his nose doing nothing to stop the deepening assault on his olfactory system. His eyes watering, he pushed through the twenty or so bodies clamouring to get to and from the toilets, the floor slippery underfoot.

When he looked down and realised what he was treading in, he almost bulked up but held it in right up until his first glance inside the loos, that's when his stomach gave in and his lunch joined the glistening, lumpen, moving, stinking floor surface. He had enough sense to vomit whilst still upright, his sense of self-preservation overcoming the natural instinct to bend down and let go.

Recovering, and in the unaccustomed brightness of the toilets, he could see fights breaking out as people were yanked from the cubicles by bigger, or more desperate victims. Doors had been wrenched from their hinges and were now just adding to the confusion as men were taken out at the ankles by unexpected broken furniture. A deep-seated revulsion at the wet shellac glazing the floor did nothing to keep folk from slipping then connecting with it. Spectacular splashdowns spattered stinking obnoxious globules of human faeces around the room, getting in eyes and mouths, creating panic and biblical spewing. Clothing absorbed ordure on contact as crawling became one of the few reliable means of escaping, of getting out of the mire. It was a stinking pandemonium. Even the air rippled with merde.

There were people squatting in the sinks, in the urinals, in corners, and the floor was awash, heaving with solids and liquids and discarded toilet paper in foul abundance. He turned away from the mayhem and his eyes fell on those that had abandoned their dignity in the urgency of the moment and were hunkered down, noisily groaning, and shitting on the corridor carpet.

Just when he thought it couldn't get any worse, he glanced into the ladies. The scene was much the same but the noise unbearable. Screams emitting at a pitch that generally only dogs can hear. Buttered and pampered legs beneath short skirts and very little underwear bore evidence of accidental and explosive gravy-coloured discharges.

Tiled diarrhoea smeared floors plus smooth soled stiletto shoes equalled zero traction and there was a tangle of shit-stained bodies where one girl had gone down and in desperation, knowing what she'd slid on and was imminently due to join, had grabbed a neighbour. The domino effect took over.

Hair, once immaculately coiffed now gleamed darkly, wetly framing faces he knew hadn't started the night wearing camouflage cream. Girls spat, the tiniest taste of shit abhorrent. There were tears and broken fingernails. And the stench.

Mitch shut his eyes and tried not to breathe. Both toilets were a war zone. Deciding that discretion was, in this case the better part of valour, Mitch decided that his first responsibility was to clear the club of punters, so he turned, rather too easily in the slime underfoot, and joined the majority, ushering them off the dance floor and up the stairs.

Closing the club had further ramifications. In pubs and clubs countrywide, there is always at least one fixture, usually found at the end of the bar. In the case of Buddy's, it was Mark. Very much a regular, friendly enough, but with a booming vocal output, Mark rarely left quietly, conversations generally revolving around an expensive tab or unfinished beer and invariably beginning with. *There's no fookin' way!* and ending with *Un – believable!*

Having enough cats to herd, Mitch didn't have time for a conversation right now so jerking a surprised Mark from his favoured stool, Mitch marched him grimly in the direction of the toilets. Moments later, Mark reappeared, green at the gills and from that point on no words were necessary or spoken and he self-policed rapidly up the stairs, beer uniquely unfinished, his mates in confused tow.

The club still wasn't clear, moaning victims proving impossible to dislodge, unable to move without prompting noisy, sporadic discharges. The rest of the interior had suffered, squelching carpets, a streaked and puddled dance floor, and walls slimy with foul handprints. The entire place was a biohazard. The clean-up bill was going to be horrendous and in his heart of hearts, Ginge figured that his insurance policy, as comprehensive as it was, wouldn't come close to covering the bill. Bar staff had secured the drinks stock and the decision had been taken to let things run their course, no pun intended.

But it wasn't over yet. Following the first cycle, a fresh epidemic broke out. In the hour or so that had elapsed since the first casualties, the NDDS taken nasally had completed its journey and the sniffers, those less impetuous or adventurous in their narcomania were beginning to go down. These now outnumbered the 'bombers.'

Some evacuees, gratefully clear of the reeking havoc that had been their night out, had swiftly but unsuspectingly made it outside to taxis and buses before being struck down. Not all made it home or off their transport before succumbing. Valet firms and bus cleaners would be busy in the morning.

Others, curious, drunk, or aimless had hung around to watch the entertainment. Amongst these a fart was heard, and the crowd scattered; some slower than others as a number began to clutch their stomachs, belatedly understanding how the first victims had felt. Fortunately for Ginge, Kim and Buddy's, they were on the street when it occurred.

In the fresh air, a solitary ambulance, apparently the only one available, blinked silent, blue reflections on the club's facade.

The pavements, doorways, shopfronts were littered with victims, all in much the same position and all with only one thought, to empty their bowels. Ginge tiptoed carefully through the mire towards the ambulance, its rear doors closed and guarded by a diminutive, bespectacled, female paramedic, and a solitary policeman, both had their arms folded, the policeman's helmet tucked out of sight. Ruth and Grant, a couple who despite their disparate roles in the community, often managed to coincide shifts, something they were grateful for tonight. How could this be explained over breakfast?

"What the fuck?"

"Don't look at us." Replied Grant. "It's happening all over. The best we can think of is to get the Fire Service out and have them hose the streets down."

"Ask them to start downstairs in my toilets." Replied Ginge, checking his shoes and trouser cuffs. There was silence as the three of them stood taking everything in. Absurdly, in the moment, Ginge recalled an old story. "Not wearing your helmet?" He asked leadingly.

Grant gripped his helmet tighter. "It's bollocks that it's for pregnant women to piss in, but I'm taking no chances."

"An urban myth then?"

Grant sighed. "If I told you it's illegal to be topless in Liverpool except as a clerk in a tropical fish store or it's legal to murder a Scotsman in York if you're carrying a bow and arrow, would you believe me?"

Ginge grinned. "Point taken. So pregnant women, policemen's helmets?"

"It's up there with being illegal to stand within 100 yards of the reigning monarch without wearing socks."

"How do you know all this shit?"

"Years of dealing with the great British public. By the way, Elvis isn't dead."

From behind her dark rimmed glasses, Ruth's eyes flicked left to right, taking in the scene. She'd closed the rear doors of the ambulance within minutes of arrival and locked them. No amount of ECG monitors, Defib kits, spinal boards, ventilators, nebulisers or for that matter anything else her unit carried were going to be of any use here and getting it covered in shit would take it off the run indefinitely.

She knew from experience that generally, diarrhoea would run its course helped along by taking in plenty of fluids and bland, low fibre foods. This was way beyond her pay grade, and she wasn't a canteen, so the doors were staying locked. She felt a stab of guilt that the very presence of her and the unit seemed to offer some people hope. Stifling the emotion, she asked the obvious question.

"Have you had a buffet running, Ginge?"

"Nope." Ginge was confident this was not of his doing; they didn't serve food. Whatever this was, it had started elsewhere. "Any ideas, Ruth?"

"None spring to mind, to be honest Ginge this is definitely a first for me,"

Arms folded, she scanned the squatting punters, reluctantly taking in the sights, sounds and smells. Then she saw him, and her eyes narrowed.

"Shush now, I'm doing triage."

She'd spotted a familiar and disagreeable figure. She nodded towards a squatting man. "That wanker's last." There was an unhinged aspect to her usually lovely manner.

"Eh?" Queried Ginge.

Without unfolding her arms, she flicked a finger in the direction of a particularly distressed middle-aged man, his trousers around his ankles and a steady stream of rank, watery fluid puddling around his shoes. He had given up and was literally sitting in his own shit, groaning, and holding his guts.

"My ex." She said softly, with a smile.

Grant looked over and sure enough, there was Gareth. Ruth's ex-husband. He hadn't seen him in the chaos. He put an arm around Ruth's shoulder and joined her in the smile.

"Jess always said he was full of shit."

Ruth looked up at her grinning partner; Grant was a full six inches taller than her.

"Mum knows best, and considering the shit he put me through this seems like Karma." Turning away she headed for the cab of her ambulance. "I'd best get on the radio." There was a spring in her step.

Shrugging his shoulders, Ginge left the policeman to crack on with whatever police officers did in these circumstances. Finding Mitch, who at last had cleared the club, toilets included, and was busy barring the door. The streets were finally beginning to clear, most sufferers now resigned to circumstances and attempting to stagger home.

"You usually know what's going on Mitch, Any ideas?" Ginge asked, his question clearly aimed at an attempt to explain the nights events.

Shaking his head, Mitch actually did have an idea at a possible cause but was keeping his own counsel. At least half of the punters had been affected. His experience was screaming that this was drugs. What, he'd asked himself over the last few hours, was the common denominator? He'd had calls from all over, other doors all experiencing the same thing, all of them completely unaware that as individuals, they'd been spared the havoc only by abstinence.

Understanding what had happened here and apparently everywhere else would eventually come through rumour and realisation and change the face of recreational drugs use for a while to come. For now, though, Ginge studied his head doorman, noting that his suit and footwear had already suffered. Gesturing at his own relative cleanliness, he spoke. "I'll leave it with you, Mitch."

"Realleh?" Perhaps his girlfriend was right, thought Mitch. It was time to retire.

PLAN B

Usually bustling with intelligence, the briefing room was out of ideas. A strategy had been actioned, and the rooms occupants were now resigned to awaiting events beyond their control. The container having been repatriated, there was an aimless standing by waiting room sense to the place. The rush to apply Adey's whatever it was to the drugs, the repackaging and redelivery had been done in the time frame they'd set themselves. What happened next would be down to the efficiency of the Albanians operation.

In an ideal world, the drugs would hit the streets en masse, but they had no way of knowing. For the time being then, it was hurry up and wait. The hours passed, kettles boiled, and cups clinked, frustrated runs were undertaken. No-one enjoyed this aspect of any operation, where they were waiting for the planted seeds to germinate.

Sacha was sat quietly next to Tom, who was engrossed in an inevitable crossword. She could read the clues but somehow resisted the urge to offer any solutions. She noted that Sid's absence had led to an unaccustomed neatness, each individual letter of a solution precisely positioned centrally in its box, meticulous block capitals in contrast to his usual, rushed scribble. While she read, the undertones of the near silent gathering continued unabated. Scratching, sniffing, a throat cleared, a radiator ticking, the muted beeps of a mobile phone in use.

With little to do but worry and think, Tom had been slumped across the dining table, his chin on his hands. The crossword disappointingly incomplete, his sluggish gaze had been pottering lethargically around the room, noting that you could cut the apathy with a knife. His mind was just idling down from riddle deciphering mode when his gaze settled on the captured phone, passed by, then flicked back in a eureka moment.

"We're missing a trick here."

The attention of the room shifted in the hope of something to replace the tedium. Ames looked up from his newspaper, Ollie stopped cleaning his fingernails, Bailey, her specs. James glanced up from his web surfing, his Billiard Room refurb was taking on a life of its own. Any fool could spend downtime in discomfort, and he had an idea that reflected a wartime Mess. He'd looked into the buildings history and had managed to find old photos and post war reminiscences that would restore its soul.

Ames responded to the remark. "How so?"

"Bailey?"

"Mm?"

"Anything in that phone about how the cash from sales gets to our boy. I mean, if the numbers are right, there's going to be a boatload of it floating about. Where does it end up?"

Standing, Bailey retrieved her briefing notes from a small desk near the whiteboard. Perching her freshly cleaned glasses on her nose, she sat and began trawling. She bypassed her background research and studied the translated script pulled from the Encrochat phone.

Bailey put down her notes, a finger tracing a line of text.

"Here's something. There're a few mentions of storage but they all seem to relate to the same location. Just where it is isn't clear. Give me a couple of minutes, I'll go through what we have on Cela, see what properties are listed and look for the most likely candidate."

Bailey left for her office. Ames revived the conversation.

"What's on your mind, Tom?"

Tom had been mulling over possibilities and one had prompted his query.

"Well, the current plan is to disrupt his operation, but we have no way of knowing how effective Adey's intervention may or may not be."

"And?"

"What's the principal aim of the drug trade?"

"Money." Answered Ollie.

"Right." Tom replied. "What if we find it and take it? Then use it to set him up?"

There was a moment where the ramifications of the idea began to settle.

"That's my man." Said Sacha, with a smile.

A few minutes later Bailey reappeared, having identified the most likely building. Her process of elimination had begun with proximity, no-one likes to be too far away from the cash, not in this trade. It was the entire point of the risks they took. Altin's properties consisted mainly of his commercial interests, the clubs, and gyms, but on a trading estate nearby, he had a storage facility.

Given an opportunity to do something, the group enthusiastically debated if an interdiction was plausible, then whether it was possible. It was. A hasty plan formulated; they got on task. They were going to bust Altin's unit. The probable outcome of their interference was overlooked, having something to focus on was infinitely preferable to sitting on their hands.

James and Ollie had observed numerous comings and goings all day. This bore out their assumption that Altin's distribution and collections system had the ability to cope efficiently with the import they'd recently intercepted and that the warehouse was stuffed with either drugs, or money. They hoped it was the latter. The Dyno Rod had begun to have an impact last night, various news outlets up and down the country reporting on a mystery illness striking down the weekend party animals. It wouldn't be long before it was attributed to cocaine, and not long after that before the dealers began looking for Altin. At the moment, Themis was in a privileged position, it wouldn't be long before that advantage was erased.

Dave drove the truck, a common sight on a trading estate and therefore unlikely to attract attention. Neil rode shotgun. James and Ollie had preceded them by car, the usual comms were in place and following their standard precautions, surveillance, and research, it was time for the incursion.

Wraith like, James and Ollie crossed the small car park and headed towards a large grey roller shutter adjacent to the main door, which was white steel, locked but not padlocked. They had more than enough time before daylight and had already discussed what needed to be done.

From earlier observation they reckoned there to be two men inside, an unusual nighttime arrangement for an innocent trade unit. The single vehicle in the driveway by the door supported their intelligence. There were no lights within or without, the cast of the streetlights insufficient to illuminate the building. The door locks were good but not good enough as silently they were defeated. They cracked the door, waiting for any automatic lighting to kick in, none did.

Cautiously, keeping low, they crept through it and found themselves in a carpeted corridor broken each side by an office door or two. The glazed top panes showed light emanating from one. Inching closer they listened and could hear a conversation going on inside. The language was, at best guess, Eastern European, and appeared to confirm just the two occupants. One each then.

They'd factored in that the original building plans would be essentially useless. The temporary nature of storage unit internal structures meant they could be tailored for each and changed on a whim. Nevertheless, they had a good idea of the size of the office from the distance between them and the external wall, it was not a large room, and having the advantage of surprise, they took it.

James tested the door, slowly turning the doorknob until it reached its stop, then, with a finger braced against the frame, pushed gently against it with his thumb. It gave sufficiently for him to release the handle with the door a few millimeters ajar. There was no sign from inside that this had been noticed. Stepping aside, he gave the nod to Ollie, who appeared to be thoroughly enjoying himself. No change there, then.

Ollie gave the door a gentle shove, as if a breeze had motivated it. From inside came a grunt of query and the sound of a chair being slid back as a man stood. Judging the footsteps, Ollie waited until the man was just approaching the door then launched himself at it. Glass shattered and shouts erupted from within as the man was propelled backwards and into a large desk. Ollie swept in, gun up, shouting "Armed Police! Nobody Move!" James was right behind him giving voice. One of the men was sprawled on the floor, the other had sprung to his feet and was scanning the room.

"Don't do it!" Warned Ollie, assuming the man was looking for a weapon. "On the floor, with your mate!"

The standing man was staring down the barrel of a gun, Ollie watched as the fight went out of his eyes and he began to assume the position. The guy who'd taken the impact from the door was less of a problem. Stunned and bruised he was barely aware of what was happening.

Both men were wearing dark bomber jackets, and these were as good as anything for the moment. James dropped a knee onto the stunned man's stomach prompting a whoosh of air and pain. Rolling him over he slipped the man's jacket from his shoulders and pulled it into a bunch behind him, immobilizing his arms, knotting the sleeves completing the arrangement.

Ollie, practiced, and not one for niceties, brought the butt of his pistol down on the back of his guy's head. Blood spurted as skin split and the man went limp. For now, they were both out of the game. The entry had been swift, brutal, and effective.

A swift body search of their victims revealed the usual pocket items, wallets, mobiles, keys with the welcome bonus of an Encrochat twin. All this was placed centrally on the desk. The two men were then pushed beneath it with the office chairs as a barricade, ensuring any movement on their part was now hampered and would be betrayed. James retrieved some gaffer tape from his small rucksack. Singly, the men were tugged from their timber prison and properly secured, hands taped behind their backs, feet together. Satisfied that for the time being at least, these boys were going nowhere, James nodded to Ollie to check the warehouse properly.

He returned momentarily, a huge grin on his face.

"In the immortal words of Chief Brady, we're going to need a bigger truck."

THE CALL

Altin was concerned. The weekend's events had bottomed out the cocaine market, clubs closed, his own among them, their clientele laid low with some mystery ailment. Well, if it was another pandemic, he was ready for it. He got paid cash on delivery and even now, that money was in the warehouse being counted, banded, and making its way to him.

Some of his own staff hadn't turned up for work today and that was a problem. The same bug had hit his gym's and there was a lot of cleaning to do, he needed his people. Now that the fresh consignment had been packaged and shipped, there wasn't much else to do anyway. The drugs operation could lie low while he arranged the next shipment and counted his money. In time venues would reopen and it would be business as usual, he needed to be ready for the anticipated upturn.

His phone rang. Not an unusual occurrence except that in this instance the screen showed the caller to be using the phone taken from the north last week. He brightened. It seemed that a problem had gone away, that the phone had been found and was something less to worry about. He hit receive and the speaker button, placing the unit on his desk, relaxing. “Speak.”

“Mister Cela.” An English accent pierced the room, it was cut, refined and alien on this network and no-one called him Mister. He was Boss. He pushed his chair back with a scrape, distancing himself from something that should be dead.

“Who is this?”

“Ah. I’ll give you a recap.” The voice was confident, composed.

“Last week, your shipment went missing for a day or so.”

Altin sat bolt upright. *Who could know about either the shipment or his delay in receiving it?*

“I’m afraid that was us. We intercepted it, jazzed it up a little then saw to it that you got it back.”

Altin’s heart was beating hard. *Was this the police, customs, another gang?* And what did he mean, *Jazzed it up*? Before he could think his way through that last sentence, the voice continued, smug, infuriating.

“You’ll be aware that there has been a slight disruption to the weekend’s usual festivities. What has yet to happen but what will happen is that the affected individuals will be found to have all consumed cocaine. Your cocaine. It shouldn't take too long for the truth to emerge and when it does, you're finished."

A sweat broke through on Altin's forehead, his imagination tried to cope with what he'd just been told. Other things, brother things disturbed his thought process. *What the fuck was going on?* The voice had said nothing since casually tossing that last verbal grenade. Altin needed more.

He forced his voice to project an authority he didn't feel.

"What did you do, clever man? Just so I know this is no joke."

"Look up Dyno Rod. You'll get the drift. Incidentally, you really should change the water in your gym coolers and while you're at it, pop down to your empty warehouse. I really must congratulate you on the efficiency of your collection system. Drugs out, money in. Seamless, and so neatly packaged. I'll be in touch." The call clicked off.

Warehouse? The drugs? They'd all been delivered. The money, that's all that was there. Empty?

Panicked now, Altin dialled his Kryetar. The call was picked up after a lengthy pause, there was a hollow silence followed by a strange voice.

"Hello?"

“Who is this?” Asked Altin, with a sinking certainty that it wouldn’t be good news.

Another lengthy pause. Before it could be interrupted, Altin swiftly shut down his phone, hit the wipe button, then set about systematically and savagely destroying the unit.

As it shattered beneath his elegantly shod foot, he thought about the first caller. He’d said the warehouse was empty, well it wasn’t. The voice that had answered his call was not one of his. It had to be the authorities and that meant whichever way he looked at it, that aspect of his carefully tuned operation had been exposed and he was vulnerable. He’d risked everything on this expansion, much of which was not his to risk. Crime was all about the proceeds. His customers could go fuck themselves, they knew the hazards of the game and if he was no longer here, he would be unaccountable. Refuge was home, Albania. And a boat packed with cash would be his passport. It was all about the money now, getting it back was his only way out.

“How much cheddar have we got?”

“Dunno haven’t counted it yet. Don’t see how we can.”

Ollie illustrated the scale of the task by opening the rear door of the truck. Filled from side to side, front to rear and piled to the roof were vacuum packed stashes of banknotes. h

“Couldn’t nick it all, we needed a bigger truck.” He offered, ruefully. “So, we called the local plod. They should have landed a while back. If our drug dealer friend is dumb enough to go to the warehouse, the very least he can expect is to have to explain where all the cash we left came from.”

“It’s too much.” Ames was concerned. Disrupting the trade was one thing, hitting them this deep in their pockets quite something else. He knew the lengths criminals went to for fifty grand. What they had here and what had been gifted to the police went way beyond that. They were going to be hunted for this.

“An Albanian gangster on a mission is the last thing we want in our rear-view mirror.” He paused, looking up at the pile of money.

“Any guesses as to just how much we have here?”

“It’s a lot.” Someone murmured, awestruck.

“I can hazard a guess.” Offered Bailey.

All eyes turned to the analyst.

“What?” She said, baffled at the expressions turned her way. “It’s simple maths.”

“Go on.” Said Ames.

“Well, if it were all in twenties and new, which it isn’t and isn’t, a million pounds would form a solid block approximately 18inches x 18inches and weigh nearly 8 stone. Even if this is made up of old notes of various denominations, some higher and lower than a twenty, it should average out. It's not like we're accountants, right? Anyway, 100 million is about 8 tons in weight. We've put the truck on a weighbridge and that's about what it's carrying. Do the math."

There was a low whistle. "100 million? Sterling?"

"Give or take."

The group maintained a short silence, the reality of what they were looking at, the sheer numbers involved, the absurdity that it had to be counted by weight blanking out everything but the pallets and what they carried. Sacha broke it.

"And you left the rest?"

"Well, most of it. I might have a bit in my pockets." Ollie dug and retrieved a sheaf of wrapped banknotes. More came from another pocket.

"I wish I'd worn my cargo pants." He grinned, ruefully.

Sacha again. "What are we gonna do with it?"

Another brief silence followed. Balance sheets were one thing, but this was a mountain of actual notes; cash money, which, in common with pretty much everyone else in the first world, was a commodity those gazing at it used less and less. What had become an abstract notion was sitting patiently on the floor, inviting sin. Simply peeling off a slack handful could be life enhancing and if done carefully, was untraceable. Temptation, the wish to do or have something you know you should not do or have and resisting it was a moral decision each was processing in their own way.

"I always wanted an 'E' Type." Ames muttered, uncharacteristically breathless. "A red one."

"Series 1 Roadster?" Queried Ollie, quietly fascinated by the pile of paper. "Oh yes." Ame's breathing was still subdued. "The 4.2"

"You could have your Bugatti, Ollie."

Ollie glanced at Tom.

"What would I do with a Bugatti?"

The group stood silently after that. Their minds working slowly through the numbers involved. The spell was broken by Christian. "It will prove impossible to launder."

Ames put his policeman's head back on. "People like Cela are rarely caught and convicted, usually through a lack of evidence, keeping their distance until the cash is clean. We need to get him and this," he waved at the pile of currency, "in the same room as the authorities. I'm working on it."

"Does it have to be all of it?" Queried Ollie, optimistically.

INFORMATION STREAM

Altin was infuriated and taking his anger out on a punchbag. The email had been cryptic but couldn't have been clearer.

Couldn't reach you on the phone. Not to worry, here we are, chatting. Anyway, I have something of yours. I'd like you to have it back. It's mobile, on a truck, in fact. 8 tons of money. I'll be in touch.

He'd tried to respond but the mail came back as undeliverable.

His choreographed hits looked and sounded good. What had once been private rehearsals until perfected, were now a public performance. The media had begun speculating on the weekend's chaos, his gym was at less than a quarter full, most of the membership staying away, his water coolers now a legend for all the wrong reasons, his fitness conscious punters now associated with drug users, having been struck down in exactly the same way as the weekends party animals. The thought lent intensity to a savage punch that sent the bag swaying on a pre-determined path, halted by a counter punch which in turn sent it rolling into another predicted path, and so it went on. He kept his feet planted, an Atlas like stance that emphasised his physique and bunched all the right muscles.

On another day, he'd have pursued the Milf on the planking mat eyeing him up. But not today. His world had quite literally, turned to shit and he was trying to work his mind through how. After the phone call that had heralded the potential collapse of his empire there'd been no contact from his guys at the warehouse, and he'd been forced to send two more to find out why.

Their subsequent report was the source of his angst. Police were swarming all over the unit and there was no way in. Altin had coerced and flattered his lawyer, even though she wasn't licensed any more, to attend the police station and find out what she could. He knew her back story, her epic fall from grace, and while knowledge was power, Altin had other means at his disposal, his light touch on her arm, a promise in his eyes, either way, she had done as bid and reported back that his on-site team had been found beaten and taped to a desk.

Two men in black, they'd said. And that was all they had. While the police had declared the discovery and seizure of a huge amount of cash, his cash, there had been nothing on, or in the news, trumpeting a successful undercover operation, which until the email, had puzzled him. So, these people were not customs, not the law, not a legitimate organisation. Were they rivals? Who were they? The frustration of not knowing initiated a violent, inelegant punch that hit the punchbag off centre, causing him to lose his balance and stumble. The Milf glanced away, nobody likes a loser.

He had the idiot who had lost the phone locked away in a trap house. With hindsight he now had to acknowledge he'd been foolish to let the Encrochat unit go on what was essentially a power play, but no matter. He would leave shortly and try to uncover whoever was behind this.

He finished his exercise with a final, heavy blow and strolled to the new water cooler.

He hesitated before serving himself. They'd been poisoned once and could be again. In his hesitation, he understood why the cocaine market was so depressed as to be temporarily unviable. The clubs, after a deep clean, were starting to open again. But no-one was getting high, not that he had any drugs to offer, and those he had sold the tainted product to were expressing themselves forcefully. His options were reducing exponentially, he had to get that money back before the wolves formed a pack and came after him. The newspapers said there was £400 million seized by the police. That meant he had the thick end of £100 million still out there, on that truck, at the end of that email, and he fully intended to retrieve it.

To further complicate matters, Bujar, his brother, was asking questions. Altin had juggled a great deal of money around. Had this operation gone uninterrupted, the sums he had gambled would have been insignificant, the reward compensating for the risk. As things stood the word 'thief' could get bandied about and Bujar was big on family honour. Filial connections would not save him. He needed that £100m, which would cover his outlay and hide the fact that any operation had even taken place, but he needed it quickly, before someone from home arrived with accusations. If he didn't recoup something from this disaster, he was finished. He stooped, reaching for the dispenser, out of habit, flexing his back muscles for the benefit of the Milf. One cup stuck to another then fell to the floor ruining his customary elegant manoeuvre, portraying him as clumsy. He crushed it underfoot.

He'd hoped to present the operation as a fait accompli, hide the full extent of the investment and maybe keep the extra revenue for himself. But now, instead of cash and kudos, he had a problem. The men in black. Who were they?

"Tyrone. That's your name, yes?"

Kreshnik was holding back on the beating, Altin was insistent on that. As much as he enjoyed the extraction process, he knew that fear of what was anticipated could be more effective than actual pain inflicted when seeking the truth. Being tied and helpless was part of the process and the teenager on the chair was tumbling out words so fast and out of order, Altin was having difficulty making sense of it until the rushed mention of the men dressed in black, the 'soldiers' who had freed Libby.

"Men wearing black? Two of them? You're certain of this?"

"Ask her! She knows who they are!"

Altin switched his attention to the addict similarly bound. Her eyes were rabbit wide, her mouth open as if ready and willing to begin talking. So far, as Altin understood it, the girl had been a tool of a paedophile ring. At some point, and he had yet to figure out how or why, their story was that she had been trafficked abroad, then rescued.

"Untie her."

"What about me?" A backhanded slap silenced the question. "Gag him." Prevented any more.

Altin knelt beside the girl and began questioning quietly, softly. Teasing her story from her. She began in confusion but as he brought her gently back and forth through her tale, it began to emerge in some kind of order. She'd been used up. Altin understood this. There were many markets for many different kinds of girls. She had been at the budget end. No longer young enough to be attractive to the discerning punter and so trafficked to the bottom end of the market. So far, so good. Her story rang true. He offered her a line of cocaine to get her mouth working, she took it and seemed to settle.

"What happened next?"

"We were in this cellar. It was hot and there was bugs. Sometimes one of us would be cleaned up and taken upstairs to the swimming pool. There'd be men, foreign men. One of them was a policeman."

"Keep going."

"Then one night, some other men came. From England, they said they were soldiers but that was bullshit. They took us to another place for a few weeks where we were looked after, it was really nice. Then one night I nicked a phone and got caught. I don't remember anything after that except waking up in this rehab place."

"Names. Do you know any names?"

She nodded. "There was a girl I knew, she was like me, her name was Lyla. Then there was this married couple Sacha and something. The two blokes that got us out were James and Ollie, at least that's what I heard the others call them."

"The others?"

"Two more blokes. Dave and something and a blonde woman. I can't remember who she was. I think there was a van, and a plane, but I can't remember."

Some more coke and another hour satisfied him that he had as much as he was going to get. The people she thought she had forgotten, she remembered. Altin now had seven names, but not much else. The rehab centre was the only solid clue, someone must be paying for that, and it was an eternal truth, follow the money.

Altin patted her on the knee. “Thank you. I have a treat for you. Wait.”

From a drawer, he retrieved the prepared hypo.

“This is very good. High quality.” He said. “Would you like some?”

Libby nodded gratefully. Her dream had come true. She’d believed she was going to die in this room and now this. She’d been useful to the main man and that always led to access to the real thing. They gave it out like sweets.

“Will you let me do it?” He asked gently.

She nodded again and exposed her inner forearm.

“I’d like you to relax.” He said. “Why don’t you go and lie down on the couch. You’ll be comfortable.”

She rose from her chair, kitten eager and crossed the room, lying down, as bid. Altin strolled over, the anticipation subduing any anxiety regarding his current situation, he felt the front of his trousers bulk up. The girl noticed it and misunderstood.

She was lying down, waiting. Altin pulled a chair into position and started stroking her hair. She gave him that look. One that said if you want it, it’s here. But the act was no prelude to sex, the texture of her hair on his hand was simply Altin’s way of remembering.

He slid the needle into her pale skin and depressed the plunger. Placing it aside, he went back to stroking her hair while feeling her pulse. He was disappointed to note that her eyes were in no way unusual, at least until they clouded, then closed. He sighed in disappointment and adjusted his clothing. He hadn't achieved his usual level of bliss while playing with her life. Perhaps because his mind was elsewhere. He stood and turned to the tied youth.

"Now for you, my young friend. What are we to do with you?"

UNEARTHED

"He knows who we are, or at least, where we are. I'm not sure, I'm confused."

"Who knows what?"

Bailey and Ames had been working on admin, the others busy elsewhere.

"Altin, he's been doing some digging, he's lost a lot of money, and he wants someone to pay. The cheque from Themis to Sandra at the rehab centre, he's traced it to us. We're registered at Companies House, at this address. PC is named as CEO."

All tiny points, little things that shouldn't have mattered, only now, they did.

"What does he know, exactly?"

The malware Bailey had installed on Altin's computer system had been feeding back the results of his online searches. Sandra, naturally, had banked and declared the cheque Ames had issued, it featured in the charity's statements and as a significant sum, had been flagged, subsequent smaller payments were similarly and properly logged.

"Well, it might not be as open and shut as first glance indicates. I can't figure out how he latched onto the charity but however it happened, its happened. Either way, we came up and he's done a search. Themis is on Altin's radar and from these search results, he's not looking anywhere else."

"How did he come to focus on Sandra?"

Bailey shrugged. "I haven't the faintest idea. Humint, perhaps?"

Ames discounted that idea instantly. Intelligence gathered from human sources. His people knew that loose lips sank ships and would never discuss Themis outside of this compound and certainly not with anyone outside the group.

"Well, he can't possibly have a source within so how the hell?" Ames halted mid-flow, of course, it was the only explanation.

"Call Sandra. Ask if any of the girls are missing."

As promised, Ames had ensured financial support for the rehab unit and Sandra had developed a line of communication relevant between a charity and its principal benefactor. On paper, Themis was a financial institution and had philanthropic interests. It was not a façade they could hide behind if a drug lord came hunting.

Bailey clicked off her handset. "Libby's missing, for longer than usual."

“That’s it then. I’ll call Arham, get a police presence at the home. Libby was out of it for the most part of the return trip, but the others weren’t. He might target them. First though, I’ll have a chat with the lads.”

Finding James and Ollie, Ames briefed them on the recent development.

“We need to beef up security and whoever you engage, you’ll need to ensure discretion, and they can’t come near the house, just the grounds.”

“No problem, Boss. Between us we know enough of our people that would be happy with gainful employment. We’ll uniform them up. Make their presence obvious.”

“Fine. But not too many in public view, that would simply invite curiosity, folk wondering what this old estate could have to hide. I’m getting twitchy guys.”

“On it, Boss.”

“I remember when we first met. I was a refugee; you remember this also?”

“Of course. And I was happy to help. It was just a small part of my work, and you know I provided my services for free. I saw it as my duty.”

Altin was sitting very close to her, and it unnerved her, not fear, more sensual. He was without a doubt, one of the most attractive of men. She tingled at the intimacy his proximity suggested.

"But your name then, it was not as it is now? Not Hutchison?"

"No. I'm divorced. Single." She added, reinforcing her availability.

"Your former husband. A financier?"

"I don't know what he does now, I don't even know where he is. I have nothing to do with him." She wanted the get the conversation back on track, about her.

"Peter Christian." He said, simply.

"Yes. What of it?"

"He is a generous man." It was more of a statement than a question, and ominous in its delivery.

"Altin, what is this about?"

He straightened; he'd relaxed her but now it was time for business. Altin felt that he was getting closer to his money, but instinct told him that there were also other answers out there. The girl's story had led him to a charity, their accounts to a benefactor. He'd spent some considerable time checking Christian and his organisation,

Themis. Companies House had provided basic information, its assets and place of business, a large and private estate mid country.

"I'd like you to look at some photographs."

Altin was nothing if not thorough and had long known that her former husband was a wealthy man and had logged that knowledge for future reference. That attention to detail was paying dividends now.

He might hang on to the rich man afterwards and squeeze him dry. Maybe even recoup all his losses, but the lawyer would have to go. The lawyer. She'd been all over them in the early years, screeching about their rights and fighting to prevent deportations. A useful idiot.

She had guided him through the UK's generous benefits and legal system, and he had humbly touched her arm and asked for help for his newly arrived friends. He knew the effect his touch had on some women, particularly those of a certain age and she was no exception, perhaps hopeful for whatever might be on offer. Once his people, the real people, his countrymen and women, got through the immigration system, he brought them under his wing, packing his businesses with people he could trust. Two of them had been busy on his behalf and the results of his research and their industry were laid out on the desk. She flicked through the surveillance photographs one by one. An imposing residence set in rolling countryside, stills of security fencing, outbuildings, cars arriving, leaving, close ups of visitors faces.

One photograph showed two men. Youthful, fit, getting out of a car. She'd bolted upright, shocked in recognition, and told him a story. Altin smiled, confirmation that he had found his thieves.

Since that moment of authentication, much had gone his way. He'd initially believed an incursion would be required, it seemed that the man sponsoring the rehab center had yet to be seen leaving his well secured estate. Then, this morning, he'd taken an urgent call from his guys watching the estate and made a gut decision. *Take them.* He hadn't even been after the woman but when his guys had called and asked what to do with a woman called Sacha? Sacha, that name again, but its reappearance meant that she was so much more than just a name, she was a link in the chain he was forging.

He'd had to fix a change of transport and dump one of his van's but that had been the only complication in what had been a rushed kidnapping, rather than the methodical, deliberate, and thoughtful methods he preferred to employ. The stupid lawyer woman had even showed them an empty house she owned, south somewhere, in the countryside and nothing to do with him. That's where he had them now and that's where they would stay, at arm's length. He knew that the clever man would call, and soon. He was very much looking forward to their conversation, he also believed he knew where he would be calling from. Everything revolved around that estate. It was time to call his people in. Show these pathetic English who they were dealing with.

A BAD DAY OUT

"Sacha, my dear."

She turned at the half heard, soft interruption. Christian had literally poked his head around the edge of the door, conspiracy written all over his face. Having got her attention, Christian disappeared. The act was unintendedly comical, and Sacha smiled as she left to follow. She saw him slightly ahead, still moving, his body language extraordinarily theatrical, his left hand held low, beckoning. The intrigue continued as he opened a side door, peeked inside and apparently finding it empty, motioned her in, closing the door behind them.

"Peter?"

His face offered apologies for the subterfuge, and he induced her to sit, drawing up a chair beside her.

"What is it?"

"Lyla."

"What about her?"

Christian shifted awkwardly, then appeared to go through some small mental torment before answering.

"I believe she has a significant birthday approaching?"

"Yes. Eighteen, next month." Fascinated now, rather than simply curious at the bizarre approach, Sacha waited. PC was not known for his empathy or emotional intelligence, and to her knowledge, hadn't expressed any great interest in anniversaries or celebrations before.

He was wringing his hands, not manically but clearly something was troubling him.

"I never…"

"Never what, Peter?"

"My chil…the twins, I was never involved in gift selection or giving. Their mother took care of all that so I've never…"

"C'mon, Pete, spit it out."

Startled by the unfamiliar abbreviation of his name, words started to tumble out.

“I’ve never bought a gift, never had to, never even considered it. I like her, we’ve become friends, of sorts, Lyla, I mean. Eighteen, it’s a rite of passage, isn’t it? The final step before being acknowledged as an adult and therefore I feel it’s high time I did, but I need help. I haven’t the faintest idea of what would be suitable, welcomed, even. Will you help me, please?”

A swell of compassion almost bought a tear to Sacha eyes. This man, this remote, formal, seemingly detached man was showing a side she had suspected didn’t exist. It was as unexpected as it was welcome. There was hope for him yet.

“What are you thinking?”

“I’m thinking we need to go shopping, you ‘n me.”

“London?” he asked, anxious not to go. Neither was Sacha.

“We don’t need to go that far afield.” She and Tom had discussed Lyla’s impending coming of age and had settled on something they thought suitable. For PC’s sake, she’d gift that selection. The two of them had explored plenty of other options. She’d sort that out with Tom later. The financier’s plight had touched her. First though, she needed to chat with the group.

“What do you think?”

“I’m not sure it’s a good idea, Sacha.”

They'd listened and Ames had expressed the groupthink.

"Cela knows about Themis. Quite what he knows is uncertain. For all we know we're being observed, it's what I'd do, given the numbers involved and what we've already done to his operation."

"Sure, I get that." Responded Sacha. "But at the same time, shouldn't we go on as normal? Project innocence?"

Ames was uneasy. The estate offered a haven difficult to broach and leaving it for anything other than essential purposes didn't sit well. He'd yet to send the Albanian another email. Perhaps doing so and having him concentrate on his biggest problem, getting his money back, would take his eye off Themis.

"Ok. But I want James and Ollie backing you up, and no hanging about. Do what you must do and get straight back."

"Don't you think you're overreacting? It's just a shopping trip. We'll be gone a couple of hours, max, and PC could do with trying out normal people stuff. The boys have better things to do than follow us around. We'll be in a public space, I'll have my phone and the first sign of anything hinky, I'll be on it, believe me."

Sacha wanted to get PC to herself, away from the estate. He'd spent too long cooped up, hunched over his monitors, hiding from the world. Some alone time would help pry him out of his little fiefdom and loosen him up a little.

She'd seen his interaction with Lyla, who would join him in his office on the top floor and surf quietly while waiting for her driving lesson, the waiting an obvious prompt that Christian responded to. The driving tuition offer was a complete surprise. Christian had a license having passed his test at Uni but not having driven since wouldn't be anyone's first choice for tutor. But they clearly had fun while they were out. Christians basic knowledge was limited to knowing how to start a car and which pedals did what. That, coupled with Lyla's enthusiasm and complete lack of fear or skill meant that Neil was constantly repairing bodywork and gearboxes.

Lyla's driving lessons followed a pre-determined route around the estate. Once every ten minutes or so, a desperate, howling engine note heralded her approach, a background noise that had Neil wincing.

Sacha viewed it as a healing experience for them both. Christians previous experience of children of any age was somewhat limited and ultimately unpleasant, but Lyla was a lively bright girl with an infectious ready smile and an approach to life that belied her unfortunate experiences of it. Sacha felt they had an affinity, perhaps because at some point in both their lives they had shut themselves off from the world. And the estate offered room and comparative safety and while at first Sacha was surprised by it, had been happy to see the man in the tower engage with something other than numbers. He needed to do something 'normal'. See the world as it is, not how he habitually viewed it, electronically. Shopping would add another string to his bow.

Sacha watched as Peter scanned the brightly lit glass cases. He glanced up, confused.

"I don't see a Patek Phillipe, a Breguet or a Chopard? And where is a representative?"

When Sacha had suggested a nice watch, she had underestimated what PC considered nice. She took him by the elbow, leading him away from the displays.

"Peter, she's eighteen, she needs something robust and practical, not something someone will tear her arm off for."

He blinked, his confusion almost total. "But it's a special birthday, eighteen, isn't it?"

"There are a few things you need to learn about life, PC. Come over here."

"A Rolex, then, at least?"

"Over here."

As bid, Christian left the glittering display he'd been hovering over and joined her.

"There. We weren't going to go quite this far but as you're hell bent on going over the top this will do nicely."

"An Omega?"

"Ladies Seamaster. Teenager proof and not ostentatious. But reassuringly expensive."

"But it's only…"

"It's plenty, Pete." He smiled, growing used to and fond of how she'd shortened his name.

Sacha called an assistant over, the display watches, the high-end ones at least, were just a polished, outer case with no movements. She disappeared to the stockroom, reappearing a few minutes later with the real thing, boxed.

"We prefer a credit card for a purchase of this size."

PC produced a beautifully patinated wallet that to Sacha looked like alligator or crocodile leather, he seemed oblivious to the environmental implications and rifled uncertainly through it.

"I have some here. I'm sure they're valid. Ah! Will this do."

The sales assistant was utterly mystified. The card had the appearance of polished steel and displayed an engraved signature, that of JP Morgan, in the top, right corner. Sacha noted that should she hone the edges, it'd be sharp enough to kill with. Aside from an electronic chip, there was none of the usual information usually found.

Looking closely at the proffered card, the assistant studied it briefly, "Just a moment," she said. "I'll check." And disappeared through an office door.

Sacha looked inquiringly at Christian. "Problem?"

"I don't have the foggiest my dear. Bailey deals with these sorts of things and from time to time they appear on my desk. Apparently, they can expire."

"Let's hope not, eh?"

Two minutes had passed when the assistant reappeared being led by a suited man, perhaps the manager or owner. He nodded to her and she keyed in the large number then handed the electronic reader to Christian.

There was a moment of confusion until Sacha nudged PC. "Your PIN number."

"My what?"

"PIN number, Bailey must have given you a four-digit number with the card."

"Ah. Oh, yes. Just a moment." Christian rummaged briefly in his wallet, emerging momentarily with a slip of paper. "Is this it?"

Sacha closed her hand over PC's. "You know you're supposed to memorise that then trash it."

"Whatever for?"

Mildly exasperated at PC's naïveté, Sacha acted. "Never mind. Here, give it to me."

Swiftly concluding the transaction, Sacha returned the card to a clearly distracted PC who had wandered over to study again the contents of the brightly lit displays. The manager/owner in close accompaniment.

Gripping PC by an elbow, she tugged, then guided him towards the door.

"If there's anything else, now or in the future, please come in and ask for me personally." The manager/owner handed over a business card, watching their departure regretfully.

Sacha wanted to make the most of this outing so took PC to a coffee chain. Being used to only the finest coffees back at the mansion the look on his face when he saw the frothy concoction placed before him was priceless. She was glad she'd resisted the temptation to top it with multicoloured marshmallows, that would probably have tipped him over the edge. He'd likely had enough civilization for one day.

It was on the journey back she noticed it, and not for the first time. A white panel van appeared once or twice too often. Taking a random turn, it replicated the manouvre, and was still in her rear-view mirror. She thumbed a button on the steering wheel. Tom answered the call.

They'd been discussing how best to bait their trap, money being the obvious choice until Tom popped his head around the door.

"Sacha's certain they're being followed." And handed his phone to James, who listened, gave advice, and handed the phone back. "Keep the line open. Ollie, Tom, with me."

Tom had listened helplessly en route as Sacha relayed events. Calm at first, the tension in her voice rose until she'd shouted, "We're being forced off the road!"

Despite shattering speed limits and Ollie's best efforts, by the time their tracker got them to Sacha's car, it was empty of life, her shattered phone on the floor, keys still in the ignition, engine running. There was nothing for it but to call Bailey and relate events. Tom got in the driver's seat; Sacha's perfume was still fresh.

Arriving back at the estate, scenarios were presented, only one of which made any sense. The stash of money in the garage was to have been used as bait, now perhaps, it was to be a ransom. No-one needed to say it. The Albanian was behind this, the new situation clear and needing no debate.

Bailey got busy. "I've accessed ANPR and street cameras, it won't take long."

Opening her laptop, she clicked on the relevant program shortcut and typed in the registration of the missing car. Daily, nationwide, around 60 million 'read' records were fed into the system, theirs would be there, somewhere. It was.

"Got them."

The first hit was some 8 miles from the estate, passing and being noted by a police vehicle parked on the outskirts of a nearby town.

"What were we thinking?" Tom couldn't help but fill the void with questions. They should never have left the compound, a shopping trip, of all things.

On a separate screen, Christian's credit card showed up as having been used at a jeweler an hour or so previously.

"There." Said Bailey. Bringing up a street camera recording. "She said it was a white van following, yes?"

James nodded. Bailey hit some keys; stills flicked across her screen.

"I'll warn Dave and Neil, we'll need to be ready to roll asap."

James nodded as Ollie left for the vehicle workshops. Both knew it was an exercise in futility to go driving off into the unknown.

You could just as easily be travelling in completely the wrong direction as the right one. Information was key. As frustrating and worrying as the situation was, they'd just have to sit tight. But that didn't mean they couldn't prepare.

Back in the Ops room, James took Tom to one side, Bailey still busy with her systems.

"We know what this is. For now, its leverage, but there will come a point when that turns into revenge."

"Who by?" Tom knew it was a dumb question, but it had been instinctive.

"That will matter later," said James. "First we need intel, Bailey's busy with that, let's leave her to it."

"Shouldn't we inform the police?"

"That won't help, Tom. We'd have too much explaining to do."

A shout from Bailey drew them back to her console.

"There's a common denominator, I've backtracked on every ANPR and camera feed, it's definitely the same van every time."

She pointed at an image of a white, tradesman's, closed panel Ford, the registration clearly visible.

"I'll track that as long as I can, but we all know that van is a 'ringer.' Eventually, if they've any sense, they'll dump it, and we'll lose them."

"Any faces we can go on?"

"There are, and there are integrated systems we can cross reference with, it's just going to take some time."

"OK. We're getting on the road, keep us posted. Which way does the van seem to be favoring?"

"Generally, south. They're on the M5."

They travelled in a convoy of two. James and Ollie with Tom in the lead car, Dave, and Neil rearmost. All were on constant feed from Bailey who was tracking the van. Lyla had posted herself alongside the analyst and her computers, fearful of the possible outcome but fascinated by the process, watching and learning.

The afternoon traffic hampered their pursuit, they could have gone on blue lights; Bailey ensured all their vehicles were on the database, but this would have attracted unwanted attention, so they stayed dark, frustrating but tactically necessary. Bailey logged the van as entering a motorway service station and then apparently, not leaving. The assumption was that it had been abandoned and that the kidnappers had acquired other transport.

It was a tense hour's drive away during which time Bailey was trying to reacquire them using facial recognition. Eventually, gratefully, they descended on the drop site, finding the van on the litter strewn periphery of the parking zone.

It was the work of moments for Neil to unlock the doors, inside was barren and clueless. Tom had regained some of his composure, recognising the reality of the situation and the fact that hysterics wouldn't help. They hadn't expected to find much in the van, but forensics might yield something invisible to the naked eye. Dave got in the driving seat and with Neil following, drove it back to the estate.

THE CELLAR

Hooded, and with some impatience and shoving from behind, they negotiated the rough, concrete stairs downwards. Night had fallen and the inside of the cellar was musty from disuse, unlit, and with the overhead lid dropped and secured behind them, fully enclosed. From above and outside, they heard their captors' footsteps receding. Removing their hoods achieved nothing but the freedom to breathe a little easier, they were in a black, windowless prison. He took the need for hoods as a good sign, he'd done the executive kidnap course and this was an indicator that the likelihood of their imminent murder was somewhat lessened.

"Who's there?"

Initially startled by the announcement that they weren't alone, surprise was replaced by recognition. Christian flinched, mentally, and physically. He didn't need light or eyes to know the owner of the question and his stomach flipped as his mind summoned up a scrawny demon from the past. He'd identified that voice instantly. It was one he'd hoped to never hear again. It's pitch grating, like fingernails across a blackboard.

"Beatrice?" The name escaped him like a groan.

"Peter?"

Why was her ex-husband here?

Confused, fearful and resentful, she'd had time on her hands, time to consider why she'd been imprisoned and how it might end. But Peter's arrival had posed two new questions. There was a hopeful notion that this was not about her after all, and cogs engaged in her mind.

First there'd been the conversation in Altin's office, engineered into an interrogation with her ex-husband as the focal point. The lawyer in her should have realised that he'd been the objective from the way the questions were phrased, targeted. She was painfully aware that Altin was not what he purported to be, her role on the periphery of his businesses getting regretfully grubbier and grubbier. So, was this kidnap for ransom? And if it was, why was *she* here? Why had Altin imprisoned her alongside her ex-husband? She could not fathom her part in this.

Growing accustomed to the dark, Sacha was kicking herself. Her insistence on the shopping trip had landed them here and she knew that their actual circumstances and immediate prospects aside, she and PC were now a problem for Themis. To add to the confusion, they were not alone in the cellar and there had been recognition between PC and the other occupant. Then it hit her 'Beatrice'. There was only one Beatrice in her world, and she could feel the emotional jolt in the pit of her stomach.

"Peter, is that who I think it is?" The question was rhetorical and conveyed with contempt and certainty. Sacha knew the identity of the voice in the dark and that knowledge pulled a trigger in her gut.

"Who's that?" Beatrice reacted, bewildered by the strange new voice, an American no less, and calling her ex-husband Peter.

Christian saw the jeopardy, the misfortune that these two women should be in the same room at the same time. The presence of his ex-wife was odd, unwelcome, and cast a new dimension to their present circumstances. Until now, he'd presumed the abduction to be motivated by money. In his world, kidnapping was an occupational hazard, Sacha's presence, regrettable. He shelved his confusion and dealt immediately with the issue at hand, they were locked in a confined space and there was no point in denying what all here would soon know to be true.

"Yes, Sacha, the other person present is my ex-wife, Beatrice."

"Who's Sacha? One of your tarts?"

"You may want to reconsider your response Beatrice, Sacha is my friend, and I'll thank you to keep a civil tongue."

This assertion confused Beatrice. The Peter Christian she knew would never have spoken to her in such a way. Nor did he have friends. Then the name, 'Sacha' began to impose itself on her, first as a memory, then as a solid voice in the dark; immediate, close, and delivered in a low rumble, as an ancient echo coming from a pit.

"Her name was Ellen."

Peter heard movement beside him, Sacha stirring, and sensed a menace that was imminent and real, and had to think fast. How was he going to quell the fury rising in Sacha, stop her from causing actual bodily harm to his ex-wife, without her feeling he was betraying her or taking sides, misdirection was all he could think of.

"Is this your doing Beatrice?"

The blunt challenge evident in the question took Beatrice aback, and in the moment she failed to recognise that there might be a more gathering threat than an apparently rebellious ex-husband. Determined to take the initiative, she attacked.

"How dare you! You started this! I've seen the photographs."

"What photographs?"

"From your estate. Two of your thugs. There was an unfortunate episode when I was hosting a seminar."

She paused, bitter reflections she'd rather forget coming to the fore. She still struggled with events, memories, sequences. Her therapist had warned her that the effects of LSD would manifest themselves in the form of flashbacks.

One of these had occurred when Altin had shown her the pictures taken with a long lens camera of activity at her ex-husband's estate. Two faces hazily emerged from the images and solidified as a memory of two incidental 'guests' that fateful weekend. They'd been there but had disappeared by the time she had come out of her drug-fueled haze. Seeing them on the surveillance pictures had prompted recollection. Other photographs showed the apparently occasional presence of the dead child's family on Christian's property, this also demanded an answer.

"And what were that girl's parents doing there? That girl's father made a remarkable recovery and I know you paid for it. I saw your 'partnership' documents during our divorce. Explain that, why don't you?"

She was beginning to wear on him, nothing could penetrate her self-absorbed, toxic reasoning. She never seemed to consider that a child had died, or the manner of it. He wished she'd shut the fuck up, which surprised him, he never used profanity, even mentally.

"I saw nothing wrong with repairing some of the damage done by the children."

"What do you mean, 'the' children? They were Edward and Verity, 'our' children."

"They were monsters. Wicked, immoral, and depraved, I'm truly ashamed of my part in bringing them into this world."

"How dare you!"

"Oh, I fucking dare, Beatrice." *There it was again, profanity.* He was quite angry now, liberated even.

"They took the life of an innocent three-year-old child, for sport, or perhaps simply because they could. Why? It's a question I've asked myself a thousand times and one you appear utterly oblivious to. That's another 'why' that needs to be asked. But by you, not me. I'm attempting to atone in the only way I know how."

Beatrice could not believe that this was her ex-husband talking. Her Peter had been passive, indifferent, caring for nothing but his numbers. He was now offering an opinion, using critical and inflammatory language.

"You." He sensed the pointing of a finger. "Your so called 'partnership'. You paid to have my babies murdered."

Christian felt a surge of anxiety, there was more than a germ of truth in her accusation, and he knew his next words; their tone, their delivery, would be analysed. The demise of the twins had not been his goal.

His initial purpose had been purely philanthropic towards the victims with a touch of mitigation for his role in fathering the twins.

The fact that Tom and Sacha had seen it through to a fatal conclusion had disturbed him at first, at least until he acknowledged a perplexing sense of relief at the twins passing.

He reduced his reply to a single word, conscious of how effectively and memorably Hamlet's Queen Gertrude had nailed a lie. He was not about to protest too much.

"Nonsense."

Sacha saved him from being forced into further testimony. She'd sat alone in the courtroom, hearing and seeing the full, sickening story defended, justified even, by a preening witch whose attempts to portray two vicious killers as victims, twisting fact, weaving fiction, had buried Ellen's unwilling role in the tragedy as effectively as a shovel.

Now, sat quietly in the dark, eyes closed, her jaw trembling, teeth clenched, Sacha flinched, as the corporate, calculating whine rolling soullessly around the cellar took her straight back to the courtroom. And she remembered the cunning picture that voice could paint, how it had suppressed the truth, contaminated justice, and felt again the bone-breaking rage she'd once used as a spur to go from bereaved mother to nemesis.

"That girl." She growled. "Was my child. Her name was Ellen."

Sacha's voice was low, but the menacing rumble at its edge knifed through the room. Christian reached for her hand, hoping the contact would suppress any further comment. Her skin was vibrating, an eruption was imminent.

"Excuse me?"

Christian felt the heat and hate rise and squeezed Sacha's hand gently. Her response was to break the contact carefully but firmly. He felt and heard her moving on her hands and knees, going towards the source, Beatrice.

"Do you remember me now, you twisted bitch." Sacha's words dripped, made more menacing by the sounds of movement in the dark, of her edging closer.

Beatrice did, vaguely. The child's mother. Her shattered presence in court had been a difficult emotional barrier to overcome when presenting her case. Since then she hadn't given her a second thought until now. Now she was an ominous presence that was getting nearer.

"Peter. What's she doing?" The polished, protected veneer of the legal professional slipped away beneath the imminent threat of violence. It wasn't enough that she'd been taken and forced into some kind of solitary confinement, a situation she longed to return to now there was fury in the room, and it was getting closer. She could feel it.

“Her name was Ellen.” Sacha repeated.

“You raised those murdering motherfuckers. You knew.” Sacha’s words dripped venom and loathing.

“I’m going to rip your lying tongue from your head and make you swallow it whole you evil piece of shit, give you a taste of what they put her through. And you, the big crusading defender. Defend my child, bitch! Go on, just a couple of words from the great reformer’s playbook. You are a vile, evil, scheming, lying excuse for a human being. I don’t know who’s worse, you, or them? My money’s on you, they were just plain, vicious, twisted fucks. But you? You thought everything through. Knew what they were, what they did, and thought nothing of it. Ellen was not nothing.”

Sacha ran out of words, of accusations but continued edging silently, purposefully forwards in the darkness.

“Peter? Stop her?” Beatrice was now unable to hide the abject terror in her voice.

Sacha’s eyes were growing used to the gloom, some shadows darker than others. She focused, adjusted, then homed in on her target. Behind her, she sensed PC groping, reaching, and she hardened herself against any interference. Her mind had gone, she was white hot, tempered by years of repressed rage. She had to get close enough to hook out some eyes, her fingers already curved, kukri like.

“I had to watch their home-made snuff movie featuring *my* daughter, you know the one, the one those incestuous little bastards watched while they were playing with each other, the one you gave them.”

“Peter? Please. Stop this woman!”

Even though he could hear the panic in her voice, it stirred nothing within him other than a need to intercede, for Sacha’s sake. He got to his knees and reached out, groping, until finding Sacha in the darkness. She was crawling, inching forwards aiming for Beatrice. He offered resistance, clutching the edge of her jacket, bringing her back.

“Sacha. My dear. Please, wait, think this through, look at our present situation, now is not the time.” He whispered “Please, come back and sit down.”

Sacha wavered, but thoughts and images demanded an exit route from her head. Rendered mute by the sheer cruelty and evil on screen, Sacha had never been able to describe the events played out in court, not even to herself. They existed as a silent movie, excerpts of which occasionally surfaced. Now though, faced with her own holocaust denier, Sacha felt the need to declare what she’d witnessed, had been forced to view, finding herself primed at last to verbally replay the images.

First Ellen missing, then Ellen found, their barren home, the trial, Tom's descent into madness and drink. The blur of her life as every day in court she watched and listened to this evil bitch claiming victimhood for the killers. Ellen a cause not an effect, *'if the child hadn't gone with them, none of this would have happened,'* an afterthought, a postscript, part of their story with no voice of her own. The lawyer bitch, their mother, had seen to that. And in the dock, the performance of those vile little shits, house-trained, impeccably dressed, timid, engaging, weeping on cue, victims of circumstance. All of it lies.

"You need to be told, Peter. You weren't there, you didn't see what I saw, hear what I heard, she was so small…and what they did to her?"

Sacha closed her eyes, remembering, narrating, her voice dull and flat. By rekindling the memories, and building on the loathing they brewed, Sacha would become furious retribution.

"At first, once she'd got to her feet following the initial hit, she was holding her arms out, not knowing why, tears streaming down her face, just wanting these strangers to stop, promising she wouldn't be naughty anymore, she just wanted to go home to her mummy and daddy." Sacha remembered her baby crying on screen, was almost paralysed by the recollection, then, swallowing hard, kept talking.

"Eddie kicked her in the stomach so hard it took her off her feet. They watched as she started crawling along the ground, trying to get away, not understanding, sobbing, so young she didn't have the words."

Sacha paused, the next images were close to unbearable, yet still she managed to continue her narration.

"Verity lit a cigarette, blew hard on the tip, firing it up. Eddie held her down while her face was being burned, scarred. Then the still lit cigarette was dropped into her open, screaming mouth."

Sacha went silent, the recollections too vivid, then dragged herself back to the present.

"Next, using the hood on her coat, Verity dragged Ellen towards a puddle, forced her face into it then stood on the back of her head, with both feet. She was balancing on the back of my baby's head, Peter. Arms stretched out with a huge grin on her face. Like Christ the fucking Redeemer."

Sacha's voice dropped. "Ellen couldn't breathe, she was drowning in mud, Peter. Her arms flapped. Her shoes hammered away at the dirt, her little legs kicking. The video got it all. They let her sit up, muddy, gasping, bloody now, crying hard, she tried to wipe some of the filth from her face, and the look in those eyes when she stared at the camera. Incomprehension. Terror." Sacha paused again, disbelief momentarily stealing her voice.

"They gave her a minute then started talking to her softly, being nice, you could see that she'd started to believe what they were telling her, that they were sorry and were going to take her home, she even managed to smile through her bruises and cuts. She had hope. She went to stand, then realised she'd dropped a mitten, her favourite ladybird mitten."

She stopped abruptly, choking on the domestic recollection, a family day, shopping. "I remember the day we bought them." Another hollow pause.

"Then her expression as she bent to pick it up, her howl when Eddie stomped on her hand, her screams when they started all over again. That was when she closed her eyes, gave up, shut out what was happening to her. It took a while, the killing. The sound of the bricks hitting her. A bit of death here, a bit of death there. The sobs receding, the breathing getting harder through the swelling. The pain of her broken ribs, burst spleen, ruptured tummy. The pathologist said that the damage to her brain meant she was probably unaware when her heart finally gave out, when it finally stopped. Her heart, that is. The Twins kept going though, long after she was dead. Ellen was a battered rag doll when they were through, they, well they were just sweaty and happy. And they filmed it all, zooming in and out, panning left and right, recording every last screaming moment of my daughter's life. The worst part of it was you could hear them, they were laughing, wondering what to do next. Discussing it."

Sacha's voice faltered, began to break, "She was all on her own Peter, *my baby girl* was on her own."

While she'd been replaying the horror, he'd reached for her hand, it was a solid knuckle expressing a concoction of agony, incomprehension, and outrage.

"And after all they'd done, this evil bitch fed them the means to relive it. Day after day, my Ellen was butchered over and over while they pawed at each other. It was the last thing those sick fucks ever saw, but she did it. She gave them the film. This is unfinished business."

Sacha broke free, she'd said enough, told enough, the memories strengthening her resolve.

"Wait a moment! Didn't you hear what she just said Peter?" Beatrice's voice was shrill with sudden understanding. In the dark. her mind had turned to all the recent, unfortunate, and until now seemingly unconnected events. His clear intimacy with this family now gave her cause to believe that not only had they had a hand in the death of her children but had also dramatically interfered in her life which had culminated in her shameful, naked rampage around a Scottish village. She wanted to scream. There was no way back from that, the eternal nature of the internet ensuring immortality.

The children, her career, its unsuccessful renaissance. Initially she had completely disregarded her ex-husband, who hadn't even bothered to attend the twin's funeral, but here he was, sailing blithely along, seemingly immune from contamination of any kind.

She got her lawyer head on, recalling his involvement with the Hoods. *Why? What for?* The mysterious circumstances surrounding the deaths of her own children, the police investigation into which had been cursory, disrespectful even, passing it off as a sex game gone tragically wrong, the looks on their faces said, *incestuous little fuckers, good riddance.* And had closed the case. She was sick of her ex-husband fawning over this woman.

Much like Tom, but for entirely different reasons, Peter had stayed away from the trial, not read any of the lurid tabloid headlines, distanced himself from the whole despicable merry-go-round. Sacha's account was the closest he'd ever come to the reality of what his children had done. The twins had appalled him then, Beatrice sickened him now. He didn't try to disguise his contempt.

"Listen to yourself Beatrice. What they were doing when their accident occurred was well documented at your disbarment hearing. Or had you forgotten?"

"There's no need to hide it, Peter. I want her to know."

Having relived the death of her child, Sacha had let go of something. All that was left now, was an overwhelming need to finish the story.

"I've dreamt about what I would do to *that* woman if I were ever in a room on my own with her. Well, here I am." Her voice dropped to a whisper. It was time for the final act.

"Nobody paid anyone. We did it for free. We killed them, Tom 'n me. You remember Tom? And you helped. We wouldn't have found them if it wasn't for you. Then we set it up to show the world for the sick fucks they were. We put the bags over their heads and watched while they ran out of air. You may have won the battle, bitch, but we won the war."

The atmosphere in the cellar was suddenly heavy in the silence following Sacha's confession. It was shattered by a scream from the edge of the room and a sudden rush of air. Sacha sensed something dark and bat like coming and dodged it, dropping to the floor. A foot struck her midriff, the flurry of activity ending with the sound of a skull cracking hard into brickwork.

RESCUED

"This is the way to…"

James interrupted Tom's train of thought. "Yes. It is."

The route was familiar, one they'd studied at length when going after the Twins. It threw up all sorts of questions, none of which had obvious answers, but they knew this road, and where it would lead them. Ollie pulled the car over into a layby, switching off the lights and motor.

Tom began, his voice hushed, this was the middle of the night and sound carries. "Are you thinking what I'm thinking?"

"Snatched and driven here, and there's only one common denominator." James said, then waited for what he knew was the obvious deduction.

"I thought we'd sorted her out." Offered Ollie. "Just can't work out what's going on. I was sure this was the Albanian. What the fuck is going on?"

"Forget it for now, Ollie." James was leaning forward, his elbows on the back of Tom's seat. "What we need are eyes on, maybe then we'll get some answers."

“Right. What do we have that we do know?”

James thought briefly then responded to Tom’s question.

“We have the three of us, the car, comms, but not much in the way of offensive capability.”

“He means guns.” Ollie translated.

James continued. “We should’ve been more prepared, but it seemed more important to follow that van at the time. As it stands, we’ve no drones, bugs, bino’s.” He paused. “Thoughts anyone?”

Tom had only one and that was retrieving Sacha. “I’ll knock on the door.”

“I don’t think so.” Objected Ollie.

“Oh, so you have a better idea?” Tom frowned. “It’s unexpected and I’ll just be a guy with a broken-down car. At least then we’ll have some idea of what’s going on inside.”

“Bailey knows where we are. We could wait for back up and kit.”

“To do what?” Tom said. “I’m not sitting here waiting for stuff that we don’t know we need because we don’t know what we’re up against. But I reckon she’s in there, hopefully with PC and at most with the two thugs from the van.”

“Not so.” Interrupted James. “All we know is that there *might* only be the two guys from the van. There could have been a few more waiting for them to arrive. We can’t park outside, we can’t stay here, it’s a country lane. Give me a minute. We’re going to have to make this up as we go.”

“Lovely.” Grinned Ollie.

Tom simmered until James eventually spoke again.

“Right, Tom, we need to reverse the process from last time. You drive, me ‘n Ollie will debus where we dropped you on your night recces back in the day, we’ll then make our way to somewhere near your old hide and try to figure out what’s what. You drive on, find somewhere quiet to sit, then wait. We’ll call when we know anything. We’ll keep Bailey in the loop. Good enough?”

Satisfied that at least something was being done, and in reality, the best people to do it were in play, Tom nodded.

Resisting the urge to smash through the four-bar timber gate, Tom drove past the cottage. His mind threw up images of their last trip here and a grim smile crossed his face, remembering the twins, lifeless in their perverse cradles. Gripping the steering wheel a little harder, the tug of Ellen’s memory and the night he’d said goodbye uppermost, he cruised on.

Recalling the drop off point, Tom braked gently, heard the rear doors open and felt the suspension lift. The boys had gone. The drop had been swift, efficient, and silent, Tom barely halting before James and Ollie disappeared. In the reflection of his taillights, he thought he saw them ghost into the hedgerow, either way, he was now alone in the car. He had to travel a further five minutes before finding somewhere quiet enough to park unobtrusively. Killing the engine, he woke up his phone and checked the boy's location. They appeared static, and off road.

Silently, invisibly, James and Ollie, recalling the aerial reconnaissance of a year or so back, made their way to Tom and Sacha's old observation point. They had a few hours before daylight and had already discussed what needed to be done.

There was no time for finesse or planning. Despite what they'd said in the car, they were going in tonight. They'd try and do it quietly but, if necessary, they'd go loud. For once, James was grateful that Ollie, assuming that firm instructions were only guidance, had secreted a pistol in the car which was now tucked into the back of his cargo pants. *I never leave home without it.* He'd grinned. They settled down for a few minutes and took stock.

There was a single vehicle in the driveway, a virtual twin to that found at the services. With luck, that indicated that the two kidnappers had yet to be reinforced. There was a light on in what they knew was the kitchen. Assuming it hadn't been changed, the back door lock was familiar though they hoped it wouldn't need picking. The rest of the house was dark. James would check the door and if it was unlocked, lift the latch and step back, Ollie was leading the charge.

A hand on the shoulder gave the signal and the two of them left the hide, keeping low, they scuttled across the unlit garden and on meeting the brickwork, slowed, creeping up to the kitchen door. Listening, they could hear a conversation going on inside. The language was, again, Eastern European, reminiscent of the money warehouse. They exchanged a puzzled expression. This was getting more confusing by the minute. First it was the Albanians, then, because of the location, something to do with the twins and now, Albanians again. It didn't matter who, what or why though, the immediate task was everything. The top section of the door was glazed, offering a peek inside.

Slowly, James raised his head until he could see the interior. Satisfied, with equal stealth, he dropped back beside Ollie. With hand signals, he briefed his partner. *Two men, seated, no weapons obvious.* Ollie nodded and waited.

As before, James tested the door, slowly turning the lever handle until it reached its full downward extent, then, with a finger braced against the frame, pushed gently. The door gave sufficiently for him to release the handle and edge it a few millimeters ajar. There was no sign from inside that this had been noticed.

Stepping aside, he gave the nod to Ollie, who appeared to be thoroughly enjoying himself. Not for the first time, James pondered again what he, Mr. Sensible, was doing teamed up with a lunatic for a partner and held his breath. Ollie gave the door a gentle shove, enough to pique interest inside. They heard a grunt of a query and a chair being slid back as a man stood. Ollie waited until the approaching silhouette solidified then threw himself into the room. Glass shattered as a head broke it, then the shell of the door caught the body and launched it backwards in a tangle of arms, legs, and furniture.

Ollie swept in, with the tried, tested, and universally acknowledged threat, "Armed Police! Stand still! Nobody move!"

James was where he should be, sweeping in from behind and moving fast across the room. Too fast for the seated man who barely rose before being struck down, James on top, a knee on his neck.

The first man had recovered and was in a half crouch near the table, a hand steadying himself.

"Try me." Warned Ollie, menacingly, then jerked the barrel of the gun to the floor.

"Lie down, there's a good boy."

But he didn't, reaching instead to his waistband. He couldn't know that despite the shouted warning, Ollie wasn't an armed policeman and really wasn't fucking about and after two rounds took him in the center of mass, stopped caring.

Ollie waited, watching for signs of life but the spreading puddle from the body said there would be none. Ollie transferred his weapons attention to the floored man. Not as foolhardy as his companion, and abruptly aware that there would be consequences to disobeying barked instructions, he had his hands and arms outstretched, shouting something unintelligible which they both took to be 'I quit!'

"I've got 'im" Muttered Ollie, his gun steady and aimed. "Go find our people."

Nodding, James left and could be heard going from room to room. He returned empty handed. "There must be a basement." At that, the prisoner pointed frantically down, and James remembered. "The coal cellar."

It had come up on their original recce and had at first been considered as a point of entry but was external and offered no way into the house proper. James knew where to find the entrance and went outside. There was a simple stick between the handles, tugging it out, James pulled the doors upwards. It was pitch black down there and James, having no torch, had to resort to calling out.

"Sacha, PC?" A face appeared from the gloom. Filthy from coal dust, a smile split the monochrome, white teeth gleaming.

Tom's phone buzzed, he listened, then beamed.

His headlamps swept the front of the cottage as he pulled in, illuminating four figures he recognised and one he didn't. The fifth was slumped, being held upright between James and Ollie. There was something about that limp silhouette that probed uneasily at his subconscious, then as the distance closed, poked through as an unpleasant development. With a *'Not now'* gesture, James instructed that Tom, Sacha, and PC take the car while he and Ollie shepherded Beatrice towards the parked-up van. He broke off to have a quick word with Tom.

"What happened?"

"There were just two of them, Tom. We'll have a full debrief back at the estate."

Tom nodded toward the mystery figure now on a back seat with Ollie. "Is that who I think it is?"

"Sorry, mate. It is. More questions than answers, eh? We'll sort it. Let's just get home."

In the car, PC and Sacha were quiet, clearly worn thin by the past twelve hours or so. Tom opted for a gentle inquiry rather than a full interrogation.

"You two ok?"

PC was stretched out on the back seat and flapped a hand in acknowledgement. Sacha was more forthcoming.

"I told her what we did."

Tom took that in. "Ah. Right. Then you knocked her out?"

"Nope. Did that to herself. Ran into a wall. Crazy bitch."

Tom absorbed Sacha's calm, almost disinterested mood.

"It's going to drive her nuts."

"What is?"

Sacha faced him, a deeply satisfied expression on her face.

"Knowing we did it and not being able to do a single, fucking thing about it."

Tom wasn't sure. "It could complicate things."

"Tom, she's a defrocked, LSD dropping freak. We, on the other hand, are a quiet, respectable, bereaved couple trying to get on with our lives. She can't do shit."

"Fair enough." Tom replied. "Feel good did it. Telling her?"

"Oh, yeah. It felt good. Reckon I'm done with her now."

He smiled. "Wish I'd been there."

"Yeah." She mused. "Me too." Then rocked by the gentle motion of the car, slipped into a gentle doze.

Hours later, back at the estate, Beatrice was secure; noisy, but secure, her head injury treated and tucked away while they waited for Adey's sedative to kick in. There had been little choice other than to bring her here but that didn't mean she was welcome, anything but. PC and Sacha had filled them in on events in the cellar.

"Our involvement," Christian gestured towards Tom and Sacha. "Got her thinking. And the unpleasant fact is, she wasn't too far from the truth. That set her off and somehow, somewhere along the way, and we think it was the same man who tracked Themis down, she obtained images of you two, and remembered you from Scotland." James and Ollie took the news with a shrug.

"What happened in Scotland?" Lyla was included in the debrief, anything else was counterproductive, but there was a lot of history she'd yet to learn. It had been agreed that Sacha would take her to one side and give her the entire story, or most of it, at least. But they had immediate issues and that would have to wait. Sacha hushed her with a promise. "Later."

"So, it's damage limitation." Offered Ames.

"We're fucked." Said James. "We can't kill her, and we can't keep her here. Eventually, we'll have to let her go and when we do, the shit will interface with the proverbial."

“Quite.” Said Christian.

“So, what do we do?”

Ollie piped up. “Why don’t we give her back to the Albanians?”

James gave him a sideways glance.

“It keeps coming up, doesn’t it?” Said Ames, interrupting the proceedings. “Albanians. This is getting messy.”

He pursed his lips, trying vainly to see where this might end but saw nothing but trouble.

“James, Ollie, sort out site security ASP.”

“Will do, Boss.”

PLAN C

Ames was plagued by doubts. He'd been sucked in by a democracy. The others were keen to see this through and he got that, he understood that by their measure, a line had been crossed. But that meant that he had to bridge a personal cultural divide, of going from upholding the law to the polar opposite. Turning a blind eye was one thing, placing a thumb on the scales another, but what James was proposing was in another league of wrongdoing, and his was a central role.

"There's no other way?"

"Not that we can see. It's not in their nature to quit and he just made this personal by kidnapping Sacha and PC. There's no knowing what he'll try next, we need to take the initiative, plan a forceful solution to our problem."

Ames looked at the map. Salisbury Plain was 300 square miles of mystery. He'd never been anywhere near it and had literally zero knowledge. He turned to James for enlightenment.

"The military have been using the place since around 1898. Most of the Plain proper has been bought up over the years, about 150 square miles, give or take. The bit we're interested in is the live firing area, around 47 square miles and prohibited to the public."

"So, no chance of collateral damage?"

"There's always a chance, Boss." James shrugged. "But it doesn't get more minimal than this."

"Ok. Keep going."

"East of Warminster and on the southern edge, is an abandoned village. I say abandoned but that's not strictly true. Lots of land within the training area was and still is leased at favourable rates to farmers for grazing and the like. A few small hamlets and villages were tenanted under the same auspices. In 1943, one of those villages was given a couple of months' notice to quit, initially temporarily, the MOD needed an urban environment to train up the Yanks for D Day. As it turned out, the temporary eviction was permanent. There's an active church still being supported but access is only granted once or twice a year. It's essentially abandoned, used as and when and given the size of our military these days and how busy they are elsewhere, the as and when is becoming fewer and further between. It's ideal."

Ames looked harder at the aerial view. There was a horseshoe of buildings to the left of the main access road, the church James had mentioned was further to the left by about 100 yards and obscured by trees from the rest of the village.

“That crescent, some of those buildings looked fairly modern.”

“Yes, Boss. Very few of the original buildings are safe to enter and an urban battleground was needed, so they built one.”

“What bodies have we got?”

“There’re the usual suspects, us. Dave’s getting on to Wes and Juddy to see if they fancy a day out, the place is remote, we need air.”

“Air?”

“I had a chat with Dave. Apparently, Wes and Juddy have a hobby. An old Westland Scout. The British Army used them for about 30 years, from the sixties to the nineties. Our boys use theirs for re-enactments. I’m told they can lay their hands on a Chieftain tank if we want one.”

Ames reacted with horror.

“Relax, Boss, no heavy armour, but their chopper is fitted with Nightsun, think of it as an airborne searchlight. Those fuckers’ll think they’re in Vietnam with that thing throbbing overhead. And when the Nightsun comes on, they won’t be able to see shit, but we’ll have a perfect view.”

Ames rubbed his temples.

“Please tell me it has no offensive capability.”

“If that’s what you want to hear, Boss.”

There was a pause while Ames processed images of Apocalypse Now.

James tried to help him out.

“People will die Boss. But it’s shit or bust. If we’re exposed life’s over anyway. I don’t know what else to say. We either stick together and see this through, whatever that entails, or we shut down Themis and hope no-one starts looking too hard for us after we’ve scattered. But there’s 100 million reasons stored in Dave’s workshop that say we’re gonna get tracked, it’s like having Long John Silver's treasure map and he ‘aint gonna let us just give it back. He knows where we are. He’ll come for us. Anyway, we’re happy in our work. Running at the first sign of real opposition doesn’t sit well. Nor do we want to spend the rest of our lives looking over our shoulders.”

Ames was struggling with the whole idea. What had begun as a low-risk enterprise destroying a drug consignment had snowballed into what James was describing as a full-blown war and as a copper, his head couldn’t get around how things had escalated. But James had a point. It was shit or bust.

“Anything else? Are 2 Para waiting in the wings? Do we have a Brigade or two we can call on?”

“Nothing like that, Boss. But we’re just waiting to hear from a couple of old friends. How involved do you want to be?”

“I have to be there, to draw him in if nothing else. I’ve been working in the Bunker with Ollie. I’ll take a weapon and hope not to use it. What do you calculate the opposition to be?”

“Not a clue.”

“Your best guess?”

“It could be the entire Albanian gangster system turning out, on the other hand, Bailey hasn’t detected any comms outside of the clique we’ve been dealing with.”

“Seems odd, that.” Mused Ames.

“Not necessarily.” Replied James. “Factions within factions, family ties, pride, arrogance. And it’s his money. Maybe he’s not a sharer. Plus, he doesn’t really know what he’s up against, who or what we are. What we can be certain of is that he’ll come loaded for bear. If we assume the worst and plan accordingly, I reckon we can cope.”

“Get things moving then. I’ll keep him on the hook with his cash as bait. I’m off to the bunker with Ollie, after that, I’ll need a chat with Adey.” If this scheme worked, Ames had an idea to lay down some smoke in its aftermath.

Ames left while James sat there thinking about their numbers. He’d told Ames that they were waiting to hear from old friends which strictly speaking, was the truth, Ollie had made contact with some mates, which was always a worry, he'd see how that panned out.

Lack of intel on the opposition was the problem. Traditionally, defenders have a three to one advantage over an attacking force. He had five professionals, six if he included Sid, a hat the old man had insisted be thrown into the ring. In addition, they had two semi-professionals in Tom and Sacha who'd killed but weren't battle tested, then there was Ames, an unknown quantity with a gun in hand, and a helicopter. If the Albanians turned up with ten or more it would be touch and go and James was displeased with the odds.

Odds, and hope. Two words James was unhappy with when planning an Op. But they were bare arsed and had too many bases to cover, that, coupled with the certainty that the meet had to get messy had left little alternative other than to cut a corner or two. PC and Lyla would need to stay on the estate and hope that the built-in security would be enough to keep them from harm. They simply hadn't had the time to get additional security in place. Bailey had stated with some confidence that Tom and Sacha's home hadn't been compromised during the Albanians online searches and they'd been clear that they were unconcerned about the property itself, but they had people there. He hoped Bailey was right, he needed Sid. He couldn't reduce his combatants and even with his ex-military contacts, saw little chance of increasing them in the short term.

Having once been part of the system, James knew that there were currently the best part of 250 private security consultancies in the UK, and those were just the ones that were registered. But they were simply not an option. The idea of starting a shooting war on English soil would take some explaining, compromise security and likely not go down well with his peers.

They were on their own.

On Bailey's advice, Ames kept it simple. Ordnance Survey maps were for the purist and the last thing Ames needed was for the Albanian to fuck this up.

"Use 'What Three Words'." Was her advice.

"What three what?"

"It's a simple system you can link with a car satnav. It'll get him exactly where we want him to be on the map without giving easily confused co-ordinates out. It's idiot proof."

Ames had his script ready. The Albanian would try to throw him with his kidnap of Sacha and Christian. He needed to make the call now, so the curveball of their retrieval could be thrown right back. But the Albanian had other leverage, he knew about the estate. Ames needed to move the focus back to the money. He dialled the number

Bailey had dredged from somewhere. It turned out to be nothing sexy, it was the reception desk at the gym.

She could have said. He thought quickly, as he rephrased his opening gambit.

"Mister Cela, please. Just tell him it's his clever acquaintance."

There was a minute while the call and a brief explanation was transferred.

"Mr. Clever Man. Please say nothing for a moment. It's my turn to speak."

Ames waited, Altin's gloating could be reversed, but he'd let him have his minute in the sun.

"Your friend, Tom. I presume he is your friend. I have something he may want back. You have something I should like returned. Now would be a good time to negotiate terms."

"You should get up to speed, Mr. Cela. As of last night, early this morning, your purchasing power has somewhat diminished. Should I give you a moment to check, or shall I continue?"

Altin gripped the handset. *Fuck! Again! How?* Clever man's confidence was too high for this to be a bluff. However, he still had dominion. He knew who and where they were. He would save that. Remain calm for now. Let the man talk.

"Go on."

"Let's be frank. This is all getting a little out of hand. We propose giving you your money back, in exchange, we'd like you to forget about us."

"That isn't possible, Clever Man. You only have one fifth of what was mine, and you've caused me a great deal of trouble."

"Granted." Said Ames, simply. "But we could cause you a great deal more, then simply disappear. Our agenda isn't personal Mister Cela, but we are on a crusade. Take your money and we'll relocate and focus our attention elsewhere, maybe on your competitors, that would be a good starting point."

Altin thought hard before replying. If they thought it would be this easy to simply walk away, they were very wrong. But there would need to be a physical exchange and he was setting up for that already. They seemed to be offering a collaboration, of sorts. He would allow them to continue with that belief.

"But you may decide to pursue me in the future and that I cannot have."

"We may, but that would be a fairer fight. I think we both know enough about each other to make life extremely difficult should third parties become involved. Why don't we just call it honours even and worry about tomorrow if or when it comes."

Amateurs. Decided Altin. How typically English, imagining that there were rules. But he didn't care who or what they were. He would recoup some of his money, squeeze the banker for the rest, and dispose of these fools before Bujar intervened.

"I agree. Where is my money?"

Ames supplied the 'what three words' location Bailey had given him along with a time.

"Make no mistake, Mister Cela, we will be ready should you decide to complicate matters. We want no more violence but will respond in kind."

Altin smiled, these people had no concept of violence.

"It will be as you say."

Ames put down the handset and wandered into the lab.

"Adey. How much of that cocaine did you say we had left?"

Altin was incandescent, his office taking the brunt of his fury. He was aware enough of his actions to ensure his computer remained intact but everything else was fair game, the chairs now matchwood, furniture upended and in disarray. Every word the clever man had spoken had been confirmed.

Of the two men who'd made the snatch, one was dead, the other babbling on about men in black. Stygian ghosts who were swiftly taking on the aspect of Gogol, the Albanian bogeyman, in the minds of his troops. The house was empty of hostages. His aces had been called and he'd been left with no cards to play. Once again, he was at the mercy of the clever man and all he could do was follow his lead. Altin did not like this loss of control over events. He called Kreshnik into the room, his Kryetar studiously ignoring the wreckage.

"The fool that started all this, he's still alive?"

Kreshnik nodded. In truth, he hadn't given their remaining captive much consideration other than to provide some rough food and water. He didn't like to second guess his boss so without specific instructions, had left him tied to the chair, the last time he'd checked, the room stank.

"We should go and see him."

Kreshnik turned, leading the way.

Tyrone had shit himself and his trousers were piss wet through. He'd stopped caring about the discomfort and smell once he'd decided that calling out for a toilet break wasn't an option. Instead, he focused on a way out. His face screwed up in concentration, he hadn't spared a thought for Paul, the boy he'd bullied, flattered, coerced and then taken a hand in killing. This all stemmed from that fucking mobile phone. The first time he'd seen it, been handed it, he felt like he'd gone up a notch, was trusted. But not now, if they put one in his hands now, he'd treat it like it was poison.

He wondered how it had all got this stupid. He'd been somebody at school, somebody on the street, shagging what he liked when he liked, handing out a bit of gratuitous violence now and then, life had been ok. He hadn't really contemplated the future, now it was uppermost in his mind. The door opened.

THE GATHERING

Sid had arrived and in addition there were two new faces in the briefing room as Ames returned. He'd been expecting auxiliaries but at first glance these two were not what he'd anticipated. Ollie made the introductions.

"Scott 'n Jules, this is Ames. The Boss."

He noticed they were wearing wedding rings. The man was perhaps 5'10", dark hair, short but fashionably ragged on the edges and appeared comfortable in a business suit, albeit with no tie and his white collared shirt open at the neck. She was straight out of the pages of country life. His attention drawn immediately to the tweed jacket and fedora worn jauntily over a crop of short, blonde hair, she even had a feather in the hat.

Already frayed by his recent telephone conversation, Ames's consternation was apparent. Moving swiftly, before Ames could say anything, Ollie grabbed him by the elbow. "A word, Boss." And ushered him into the corridor.

"What the?"

"Appearance can be deceptive, Boss."

"Appearances!" Sputtered Ames. "We need operatives, not the village power couple!" Ames thrust out an arm, pointing down the corridor. "What are the odds that if I go and look in our car park there'll be a jaguar estate sat there with a couple of spaniels in the back?"

"They've been working, come straight from a job, as it happens. And it's a 4x4, no spaniels."

"What kind of job? Banking? Selling industrial machinery? And how is it that you lot are all around the same age? Is it a club?"

Ollie stepped back, hands outstretched, palms upward. He needed to slow Ames down.

"They're up there with the best in the business. The fact that you've taken them to be what they appear to be just confirms that."

Ames's expression softened. "Keep talking, Ollie."

"We're of an age because our generation has seen Ireland, the Balkans, Iraq, Afghanistan and a few more besides that don't get talked about. We go with who we know, people that were there with us, so yes, it is a bit of a club. Jules is ex Recce Regiment, served with Bailey. Was her superior in fact, until Bailey shifted to IT. Scott, he was one of us but ended up working alongside of her. He liked what he saw and opted in. They've been private for a while now. High end celebs and the like. They blend in."

Ames had calmed down sufficiently to realise that his overreaction had been due partly to stress.

He took a deep breath. "OK. What do I do now?" He asked, painfully aware that he hadn't given a good first impression.

"You'll be fine. Just go in and say hi. They're used to being underestimated."

They were standing as they had been, side by side, exchanging pleasantries with Bailey and James, going through proper introductions to Tom and Lyla.

"Apologies." Said Ames, as profoundly as he could. "I understand you're actually stone-cold killers."

The woman, Jules, broke into a wide smile.

"That's alright Bab, just don't tell Beyonce." Her accent betrayed her origins as somewhere around Birmingham. Further pleasantries were cut short as eyes cast skywards, as from outside, the unmistakeable sound of an approaching helicopter broke the awkwardness of the moment.

"That'll be Wes 'n Juddy." Ollie led the way, keen to cast an eye over their 'air force'.

Perched on the lawn, the Westland Scout posed like something from a 1970's recruiting poster, its rotors whining slowly down.

“Fuck me. The last time I saw one of those was in the desert.”

Wes and Juddy were standing proudly beside their ‘hobby’. Wes resplendent in shorts and a floral number clearly designed by a blind Hawaiian, and Juddy in his customary cord trousers, collarless shirt, tweed waistcoat and flat cap. The aircraft itself was all rivets and fresh, olive drab paint.

“Get stuffed, Ollie.” Juddy gently stroked the flank of the aircraft. “This little beauty has earned her spurs.”

“Where’d you get it?” Ollie was walking around, clearly dubious.

“At auction.”

“Mad. You’re both fucking mad.”

“Where’s the back seat?” Bailey was now investigating.

“Took it out. Saves weight.”

Bailey glanced at the two men, then into the tiny front cockpit. Looking them up and down, she politely refrained from suggesting other ways of reducing the overall tonnage of the aircraft. Ollie didn’t.

“30 years ago this thing would carry six. I reckon that’s down to four.”

“Nasty bastard.” Juddy countered. “Since we got our hands on it, we’ve basically replaced or rebuilt the airframe, rewired her, fitted a brand-new crated engine we liberated from storage. Now look at her. Not bad for a 60-year-old.”

“Trigger’s broom.” Ollie remarked. “Had 5 new heads and eight new handles, still looked like new.”

Wes beamed. Raising his index finger, he mused. “Note to self, aircraft just christened. Find signwriter.” Juddy nodded, “Works for me.”

James intervened. “Any issues with it? It all works, right?”

“Runs like a watch.” Stated Wes, with some finality.

“Assuming you hit the right switches.” Added Juddy, with a pointed glance at his co-pilot.

“A technical hitch.” Wes countered. “My fingers ‘aint as dainty as they used to be. They should never have put the cabin heater switch next to the fuel shut off, nor should you,” He jabbed an accusing finger at Juddy, “have replaced the original with a toggle switch from a 1960’s Triumph Herald.”

“In mid-flight!” Juddy expressed horror to the group. “He’s cold, and does what any normal human being would do, switches on the heater, except it wasn’t, was it, Wes? I’ve never enjoyed the counter rotation experience as the engine switches off, it makes for a hard landing."

"Sorry, old lad. No harm done."

"You fitted a switch from a Herald?" Ollie asked, in disbelief.

"It had a nice patina." Juddy countered. "And anyway, I couldn't find an original that worked. Seemed to me that it was at least from the right era."

"I assume it has an airworthiness certificate?" Given its intended use and the replacement parts issue, it was an incongruous enquiry, but Ames couldn't help himself.

"Never had one, doesn't need one. Military, see? Got an experimental cert, though." Ames gave up.

"We could be here all day talking about the origins of the history and politics of the region, so we won't. We're more concerned about the level of violence these guys are capable of. If we have to talk about history, and up to a point we do, it's a mess and as usual, about sovereignty. Kosovo declared its independence from Serbia which was itself part of Yugoslavia. Kosovo's southern border is with Albania, its population 90 plus percent Albanian. Serbia unhappy, ergo, conflict. Ethnic cleansing, blood feuds, Albanians killing Serbs, Serbs killing Albanians, both sides killing their own, either way these people have form and experience. We have no way of knowing at what level our guy was or is a participant in any of that but what I can tell you, with absolute certainty is that they neither forgive, nor forget. These guys know how to bear a grudge. It's in their DNA."

"So, we've no choice?"

"Well, we could run and hide, any takers?"

There was silence in the room.

"Bailey's right. We have no choice. But this is getting way out of hand so when this is done, I'll be resigning."

"Boss?" Asked James, breaking the stunned silence Ames's final words had caused.

"Themis began as a force for good. We're now in the situation where we appear to be planning an all-out war on British soil. I'm no soldier, I was a policeman, in many ways, I still am. I'm still here only because the security of the group is threatened, under any other circumstances, I'd be tending a garden somewhere sunny."

James understood the ex-policeman's viewpoint. This was getting heavy and as a soldier, he was used to an escalation in positive action. But there was something he needed to say.

"Boss. I get it, I really do, but we didn't start this. All we did was interrupt a flow of narcotics. Under normal circumstances, with the kind of criminals this country is used to, everyone would move on.

But not these people. They've imported a level of barbarism that can't be ignored. They don't care about uneasy or unofficial truces between the law and the lawless. They only have one way of dealing with the likes of us and it doesn't include taking their lumps and walking away. We must fight fire with fire, or they win. To beat a bandit, you gotta become a bandit."

"I know." Agree Ames reluctantly. "So how do we do it."

James stood and made his way to the whiteboard. There was a map secured to it.

"Some of us know this place of old." There were nods and grunts of assent around the room. Most of them with a military background had spent weeks training on this urban battleground and not all of that time was remembered fondly.

"You can see it's essentially a small village with around twenty buildings in a central area, with a church to the west, a farm or two to the north and a manor house to the east. There's a layby just south of the houses and that's where we hope our visitors will park, it's the location they've been given. You'll also note the hedgerows and ditches close by to the south and southeast. That's where most of us will be, behind them. Once things kick off, hopefully they'll naturally seek cover in the buildings, this is where we take our tactics from terrorists. We'll set IED's and likely take out a few. Any left will be stuck between us and fear of further booby traps, those we'll have to winkle out, one by one. Any that escape the house to house will run northwest, towards the open countryside. We'll have a cut off team there."

"Any idea how many? What kit they've got?"

"Not a clue, we'll assume they have all the goodies, NVG's, thermal imaging, the whole nine yards and plan accordingly, after that all we can do is bomb up and hope for the best."

"It'll be noisy." Said Ames, aware that this was England.

"It's MOD property. The entire area is closed to civilians who are regularly warned about unexploded ordnance lying around. The locals are used to bangs, flashes, and the occasional helicopter."

Wes and Juddy brightened. "What are your plans for us, old lad?"

"In the first instance, blind them with Nightsun, disorient them with noise. Lastly, if it comes to it, Casevac for us. Ignore them."

Tom raised a hand.

James addressed the obvious query. "You and Sacha are the cut off. That's the way it has to be, urban battles probably aren't your thing. Me, Ollie, Scott 'n Jules will be the ambush group."

James addressed Sid. The old man looked, hard, mean, and useful in his ops gear. "Any preferences?"

“I’ll just wander around the rim, tidying up.”

“Works for me.” Replied James. “But wear a hat or something, we need to know who’s who.”

Sid nodded. Dave chimed in, looking dubiously at the weapon Sid was cradling. He’d recognised it as an old school 7.62mm Self Loading rifle, or L1A1 SLR. Originally designed in the fifties, it had seen service until the eighties, this one though, Dave noted with a practiced eye, was subtly different.

“What’s that?”

“This old thing?” Sid held the weapon up for scrutiny. “From down under. We knocked a few inches off the length of the barrel and made our own straight, thirty round mag rather than you Poms and your twenty. Our lot used ‘em in Vietnam. Proper firepower. Snuck it in during the seventies. Been under my bed ever since.”

Dave noted that the butt, stock, and pistol grip were wood, not polymer, as used on later models. This was almost an antique.

“You sure you don’t want something a bit more modern?”

“Nah.” Sid drawled. “Me ‘n this old bitch are mates. I’ll stick with her.”

That debate over, the briefing continued.

“What about me?” Queried Ames.

"Ah." Said James, pausing for effect. "You'll be on the phone, Boss. Front and centre, with the truck. Bait. Bailey will be inside the back of the truck, just in case."

Ames was tempted to ask what *just in case* meant but instead, nodded. "Is there a bulletproof vest available, in my size?"

Tom and Sacha wore their old, faded and worn black ops gear like a second skin, glad they'd kept up their fitness level and that it still fitted. Lyla stood with them, awestruck.

"Wow. Parents evening will never be the same."

"We don't do those, honey," Sacha replied. "Home schooled, remember?"

Lyla smiled. "Can we talk about that when you get back?"

Tom took hope in her optimism. This wasn't the observation worked they'd trained for. Sacha carried the 'long', a sniper scope fitted. She'd been in the bunker on the pipe range, zeroing it as best she could in the time available. Both wore their pistols and were equipped with night vision; they would be nowhere near the helicopters operating area having selected a hide on the most natural escape route. They'd be hiking there from the drop off.

Sacha crooked a finger at Lyla. "Girl time, honey." They wandered off to a quiet corner, deep in discussion.

Across the room, James, Ollie, Scott, and Jules were similarly clad and equipped less the sniper rifle. Ollie had an M4 Carbine with an M203 Grenade launcher attachment fitted and a bandolier of grenades over his chest, the remainder carried L129A1's, a 7.62 NATO designated semi-automatic sharpshooter rifle, fitted with Trijicon Advanced Combat Optical Gunsights or ACOG, and good up to 800 metres. Dave and Neil were at a trestle table, putting the finishing touches to what were essentially, IED's. Sid sat quietly, a dark keffiyeh hanging loosely around his neck, charging magazines. All carried pistols according to preference. They were bombed up.

VILLAGE LIFE

This was bad. He knew the vest they'd put on him was a one-way ticket taking him to somewhere he'd never been before; to deliver a bomb to people he didn't know, from people he didn't know. Tyrone was shitting himself.

He was tied to a chair, in the room with him there were around twenty men, all foreign, the only two faces he knew were of the pair that had tortured him. The inside of the brightly lit industrial unit was a hive of activity. Trestle tables embellished with more weaponry than Tyrone knew existed outside of Hollywood meant only one thing, that someone was preparing for war.

"We are clear?" Altin had the attention of the assembly. "They have no idea what's coming. We kill everyone, all of them. We leave no-one behind."

Altin wasn't referring to the military ideology, this wasn't about dead warriors being repatriated home for a ceremonial burial. This was about clearing up, punishing those that had dared to cross him, there would be no survivors. His hands would be clean, and the rebuilding could begin. The clever man had chosen an old military range. Not so clever. It gave Altin a free hand to bring down fire and pain on the heads of those who had chosen to challenge him. They would not live long enough to regret it. He would turn the wasteland into a killing ground and walk away. Altin had brought together every one of his Kryetar's, all his loyal Albanians and had gathered them here with all of the tools required. Ak's, Uzi's, automatic pistols, revolvers, and some grenades he'd never thought he'd be able to deploy. A table filled with prepared Molotov cocktails completed his arsenal. It was like the good old days back in Kosovo. He wondered what blood group the clever man was. He would be happy to sell pieces of him on.

Moonless, cloudy, pitch black, it was the silence that unnerved Ames. Part of him was comforted by the knowledge that in this partial vacuum the approach of the Albanians would be heard from some distance, their night sight would be compromised, accustomed to the use of headlights, their hearing untuned to the night. His people would be ready.

He saw the sweep of headlights long before he heard the approaching vehicles. There looked to be an awful lot of cars, that meant a lot of the enemy incoming.

James, head down in the ditch with Ollie beside him, waited as the convoy swept past. Sid was prowling the village, Bailey was inside the truck, he'd positioned Scott and Jules on the other side of the road, Dave and Neil were slightly up range, concealed out of arc where he figured the cars would stop opposite the layby. He'd set this up as a basic triangle. Behind Ames and the truck, set slightly inside the village, he had a decoy car with its engine running and false thermal images of people inside. He and his people were under thermal blankets. If the Albanian had night tech he'd see only what James wanted him to see.

Altin's satnav, wired in to the 'what 3 words' locator, led him the layby he'd seen on an aerial map courtesy of the internet. There was no room for all 5 cars, but he let the one's to the rear worry about that, pulling in and nodding to Kreshnik.

"Arm it."

The sweat on Tyrone's brow was nothing compared to the dampness that spread from his groin down the cloth of his trousers. He'd tried begging, pleading but had received nothing in return except pain. He felt the man's hand fiddling with the vest, heard a pin being pulled, saw the remote control. Ahead, illuminated by headlights, Altin saw a large panel truck and a solitary, overcoated figure standing beside it. He dialled a number then watched as the lone figure responded, raising a handset to his ear.

"Mr. Clever Man." He spoke softly into the mouthpiece.

"Five cars Mr. Cela. Do I worry you that much?"

"I should. I should have worried you before you interfered in my business, but it's too late for that. I'm sending my man over, to check you have what I want."

The cars emptied, men dispersing loosely around them. Altins thermal imager showed a heat source behind some houses to his front, clearly a vehicle, a car with people inside it, it's running motor glowing softly. There were no signs of other life. The clever man was nothing of the kind, but an idiot, and his men soft and stupid, staying in the warm with the heater on instead of deploying, imagining that this was to be a fair fight. His British sense of fair play clearly hadn't anticipated the Albanian culture of revenge, hakmarjja. He would never get back to his car.

"Send him."

Tyrone heard the click of a door handle and was pushed out into the chill, he stumbled, then remembering what he was wearing, quickly steadied himself, as if the bomb going off early was going to be a problem. Kreshnik took him by the arm and led him forcefully towards the truck. Behind him, Altin moved to the rear of the convoy, it was time to disperse his men. He sent four to stand by his car, the remainder he drew into a huddle.

"Kreshnik will leave the fool in the vest to stand between us and the truck. When I trigger it." He raised the remote control, "Be sure you are in cover and ready to move when it blows."

From his vantage point, James's brow was troubled. Even from here, he could see that the smaller man in the bulky jacket was being pulled unwillingly, he seemed to be cringing. The Albanians were taking cover. Even considering their circumstances, something wasn't right.

He called in the helo. "Light him up."

Wes and Juddy had been hovering out of sight and sound, waiting to haul on the collective and join the party. They arrived noisily at two hundred feet as the two walking men were halfway between the convoy and Ames.

Juddy flicked a switch and the 30-40 million candlepower Nightsun searchlight designed to illuminate from a typical range of 3000 feet shone down like an alien tractor beam and blinded everything that had automatically looked up on hearing its approach. Kreshnik bolted, running in retreat towards his compatriots. The lone, transfixed figure tried to shield his eyes while sinking to his knees and it was then that James recognised the eccentricity of the man's behaviour. He'd seen it before, just once, at close quarters and had barely survived the encounter.

"Suicide vest! Take him out!"

The instruction had gone out over his throat mic.

James opened up with his carbine, and he wasn't alone. Six weapons trained on one target made it inevitable that there would be a strike.

Had Altin used plastic explosives, nothing spectacular would have occurred as C4 is incredibly stable and a bullet passing through it will have no effect; it demands a specialised detonator. Terrorism has its drawbacks though and while Altin had access to bomb making ingredients, they were anything but stable. The TATP, Triacetone Triperoxide home-made explosive that Altin had employed in the suicide vest contained a lot of oxygen. Expose that to the effects of a supersonic heat source and the results are remarkable. In Tyrone's case, once initiated, there was a spontaneous chemical reaction driven by a large exothermic modification. This initiated a swift positive entropy change which in turn, expanded rapidly at a burn rate of 22,000 feet per second, vaporising Paul's classmate and completely easing his worries of a premature detonation.

Tyrone barely registered as an entity in the destructive path that erased Altin's car, blasting it sideways, upwards, and outwards, dismantling the four men he'd detailed and shifting some of the other vehicles on their suspensions.

The helicopter stuttered in the air, blown upwards by the shock wave, its rotors flexing and ineffective, the force of the blast the only thing keeping it airborne. Wes could sense the tips of the rotors fluttering as he wrestled to control the machine, the beam from the Nightsun darting like a laser through the night sky. They were fortunate that the blast was designed to go sideways and not vertically, or they and their machine would have been toast. The fire from the lead car was sufficient illumination as regaining some control, Wes heaved the aircraft on its side and reluctantly left the fray. A downed Scout would only add to the confusion.

James felt the heat on his skin and debris scatter and strike around him. Spectacular as it was, he'd seen larger and more destructive ordnance go off and noted gratefully that there were no ball bearings to add to the carnage, just bits of meat. It had clearly been designed to cause chaos rather than mass destruction. It was time to add some of their own. Glancing sideways at Ollie, who was ruffled but unhurt, he spoke again.

"Knock yourself out, Ollie."

Bracing his left hand on the magazine, and taking up the tension on the forward trigger, Ollie let a 40mm grenade fly. The dull plop it made on exit was nothing compared to the roar as it hit the rearmost car. The men that were slow to react to the unannounced vest detonation suffered for it as more flames and confusion shattered what was left of the night. Men went down, some for good. Altin, his trap identified and invalidated, suddenly and supremely aware that he may have underestimated the clever man, had taken to his heels with

Kreshnik and others following. Rounds were coming in from all sides and more of his men fell. Several of the swifter ones had made it to the shelter of a building. Altin had been looking to his rear and only felt the explosion from the IED the runners had triggered on going through an inviting doorway. Sweating, cut and grazed, Altin cast around. This was not his first time on a battlefield and those survival instincts kicked in; every sense opens all at once, communicating the nuances of the carnage, the tiny details that were the difference between life and death. Computing the results, he abandoned his men and headed for what appeared to be a church, calculating that there were some things an Englishman would never violate with a booby trap. The murder going on behind him would mask his departure. He would disappear, hide, and wait.

When the lone, cowering man had detonated in a riot of noise and concussion Ames had been blown off his feet, something had struck him down and he sensed injury, felt blood. Rounds from Ak's crackled in the air, but they were largely unaimed and simply the result of a live reflex or a dead trigger finger spasm as he rolled for cover beneath the truck, hearing the roller shutter above him open as Bailey joined the fray.

The convoy was a flaming wreck, stowed Molotov's adding to the conflagration as petrol tanks strained and heated beyond design criteria erupted sending haphazard and deadly tongues of fire in all directions. Tyres exploded, glass shattered and choking fumes poisoned the atmosphere. The more fortunate men scattered, the unlucky lying still, inert, despite the chaos. Ollie had continued charging the grenade launcher, mad keen to get off as many rounds as possible, all aimed at the vehicles, before James called to check fire.

Ollie felt a tap on his shoulder. "There!" James shouted. "Pop one through that window!"

Some armed individuals had escaped the ambush and had taken refuge in one of the three buildings James had left untouched. Booby traps are notoriously unreliable and indiscriminate, owing no loyalty to their creator. James wanted certainty, and kettling any survivors would increase the odds of that happening. Ollie grinned and re-aimed.

The ground floor blew out and the top floor and roof dropped in on it and its occupants, dust from the demolition completely obscuring the scene. Reluctantly, James concluded that from this point, house to house was the only solution and gave the pre-agreed instructions over his throat mic. Firing ceased abruptly, in the last few seconds it had been noisily one-sided, the opposition either dead, out of the game or hiding. It was the last two categories that needed to be sourced and dealt with. He could hear magazines dropping from weapons and fresh inserted, saw his companions rise from their concealed positions and go through their drills.

Altin had made it to the church. Shocked at the firepower that had been brought down he needed a minute to evaluate, he needed concealment so he could think, had to have time to take stock. He still had a card to play, he may yet survive this slaughter. He considered his options and the odds. He had his weapons, an Uzi and a sidearm. Doing a physical check, he established that though cut and scraped, he was as yet uninjured. His wits had been addled but were now functioning again and he had his phone, and options on the other end of it. He settled down to wait.

Ames was still beneath the truck. He'd yet to get up and lay motionless. Bailey, protected by the bulk of the vehicle was partially deaf but otherwise unhurt. Crouching, she shouted at the prone figure beneath the truck.

"Are you OK?"

Nothing.

"Boss! Are you ok?!"

She saw movement. "I'm not sure." Came a hesitant and subdued reply. "I felt a hit and went down, after that I may have passed out for a minute."

Bailey scrambled beneath the chassis to where Ames lay. He remained still while she did an extremity check. Finding nothing of note bar torn trousers, she touched his shoulder.

"You're still in one piece, Boss, but I need to check for holes. I can't do that here; I need to drag you out."

She saw and felt his head nod and grabbing his coat collar, rolled him onto his back and with scrabbling heels, pulled him out into the open. His face was bloody from a deep cut on his temple, other than that, he seemed intact. She explained what she'd found as she applied a field dressing she'd taken from Ame's pocket. Everyone carried their own MiniMed pack, and you always used the casualties own kit first.

"That would explain why you might have passed out!" She shouted. "How many fingers?"

Ames counted the raised digits. "Three! It's always three."

She smiled, first at his ability to focus, and second that he still had a sense of humour. "OK. You're good to go." From the corner of her eye, Bailey had glimpsed a fleeing figure go into the church. "Boss. You up for this?"

Ames nodded, sleeving blood from his face. The dressing had stopped the flow, he just needed to clear his vision. Bailey helped him up but after that, he was steady, his balance good. He retrieved his pistol from his pocket and followed Bailey's lead.

The church door was ajar, the interior damp with just a little light reflecting colourfully, kaleidoscope like through the stained-glass windows from the fires outside. Ames tried to shut out the shouts, snaps of fire, sounds of combat coming from the houses, he needed to concentrate on who was inside and already seasoned, eyes and ears adjusted to the interior. Bailey led, creeping low through the door gap. She went right, so Ames automatically went left. The church was surprisingly intact and there were clear indications of recent use. Then Ames recalled that once or twice a year, the village was open to visitors, the church a central part of the experience. It was looked after, still consecrated.

"Is that you, clever man?" The sudden breaking of the silence caused Ames to start. He settled as the words echoed hollowly around the large void above the nave.

Ames took a moment. His voice needed to be steady, confident. "Mister Cela. You were not faithful. Who was the man in the suicide vest?"

"Not important and as for faithful? I admit, you were not intended to survive our encounter. But look at what you've done, clever man. You have created many widows tonight, many orphans."

Ames heard theatrical tutting. "This is not very English, my friend. Not cricket."

Ames allowed for a little silence, then he sensed rather than heard Bailey creeping forwards. He needed to give her time. Being Ames, once their main adversary had been identified, he'd studied some Albanian culture. Not for the first time, he blessed his inquisitive nature.

"Perhaps not. But every man is the maker of his own fortune. Yours deserved what they got, as will you."

"Ha! You throw my own country's proverbs at me." There was an abrupt silence broken by a threat. "Whoever that is coming my way, I would stop where you are."

Ames heard the tiniest shuffle as Bailey responded to the challenge.

"I have something that will interest you, clever man. I intend to leave here tonight, alive. You should listen."

Ames felt alarm. Then as calmly as he could, responded. "Which is?"

"Not all of my friends are here with me. Some of them are elsewhere."

"Tell me, then maybe we can talk."

"But we're talking now. I'd rather negotiate. If my money really is outside, I need the keys for that truck."

The conversation echoed eerily around the near empty church. Ames noted a confidence in the Albanians tone. There was no other option other than to listen.

"Negotiate away."

"Ah. But I don't know what I have yet. I'm waiting to hear."

"Hear from who?"

"My friends."

Cela was starting to irritate Ames. Either he was playing for time, or he had something to bargain with. Ames needed to know which.

"Get on with it, Mister Cela. My companion has limited patience and is very good at what she does. She's yards from you."

"Aha! A lady. How nice. In another time, in another place, our encounter might have been perhaps more romantic than present circumstances allow."

Bailey didn't respond. She knew this was a hook baited for her, that Cela wanted to know where she was. The silence stretched as Altin waited for a reaction and Ames an answer.

"Mister Cela. She's getting closer." Ames threatened, he needed to move this conversation on. He heard a shifting of position, not Bailey, he concluded, the Albanian.

"Then she should stop. Or your friends at your headquarters will pay."

Ames stifled a groan. If it was a bluff, it was a good one. Ames decided to call it.

"Who do you think you have, Mister Cela."

"Ah. Well, I can't really say. I'm waiting to hear. You don't really think that I could be certain my money would be here. But I had to come because it was where you would be and I very much wanted to meet you. So, some associates of mine are taking the time to have a look around your house, clever man. Perhaps you can tell me what they'll find."

There was the sharp scrape of furniture being dislodged. In the gloom, Ames noted that Bailey had in fact got within a few yards of Cela but was now running in a crouch, rushing back to where he hid. There was an urgency to her every movement.

"The chopper." She hissed. "Everyone's busy clearing house. If you can manage here, I'll get airborne, grab Tom and Sacha, and get to the estate."

Her eyes urged him for an instant decision. It would mean he would be here, alone. For a moment he wavered, then nodded. He hoped Bailey hadn't seen the indecision for what it was. Fear. If she had, she gave no indication, before bolting through the door.

"So, clever man. It's just you and I now."

Ames heard a shuffle of movement; he resettled his pistol in his hand and waited.

"Fuck me! Did you see that?"

Of course she'd seen it but knew Tom's words were an automatic reaction to the ball of fire some half a kilometre to their front. The thundering bang was almost instantaneous.

Sacha nodded and settled down behind her scope. If anyone was coming their way, she'd be ready for them. The night breaking open wasn't the signal they'd expected but it was clear things were now in motion. Her thumb sat easily above the safety catch and steadying her breathing, she waited.

Dave and Neil emerged from their ditch. The firefight had been brief, brutal and up until now, one-sided. Both had emptied a full magazine into a cone of fire, concentrated on the larger group to the rear of the convoy. There was movement, but not much, and definitely not aggressive, their targets were down. They crouched and began the run towards the bodies. The work would be unpleasant but was required. The downed men had made a conscious decision, and it was not going to end well for them. Witnesses were, regrettably, unacceptable. They slowed warily as they neared the jumbled disarray of carcasses. All movement had ceased and there was silence. Dave moved towards a smouldering vehicle, one slumped figure half in, half out.

Pyrolysis. The decomposition of a substance by heat, a build-up of flammable gases within a tyre creating an instantaneous pressure of 1000psi that leads to a rupture or explosion. Most tyres will blow at 200psi, but the simple speed of pyrolysis takes the rubber way past that before spectacularly disintegrating. The danger area can be up to 300metres. Dave and Neil were much, much closer than that. When the tyre blew, both men were knocked off their feet. Dave by the force of the explosion, Neil by Dave being cannoned into him. Stunned, in the most precise sense of the word, it took a moment or two for the men to stir.

"You alright?"

"Fucked if I know. Got something in my eye."

It was the tiniest thing. The smallest fragment of rubber travelling at colossal speed had struck the dead centre of Dave's right eye. It penetrated the cornea, the iris, the pupil, the lens, passed through the vitreous cavity before settling perfectly on the optic nerve.

"Come on, Bird. Time for some housekeeping."

"You know it annoys the shit out of me, what kind of nickname is that anyway?"

"Oh, pull your big girl pants up Scott. Work to do."

Cautious and wide awake, Scott and Jules ate up the ground between their lying up position and the blown house. Mindful that they had friendlies around, trigger fingers were across the guard but very, very ready. Jules was ahead, it was her way, so not for the first time, Scott was covering her back, scanning forward, left, right, glancing behind. She was a few yards ahead and had ducked out of sight around a ruined corner of twisted timber and disordered broken brickwork. Shots rang out.

"Shit!" Adrenalin pumped sweat broke out bodywide as Scott raced to get eyes on. Rubble shifted beneath his boots, and he stumbled, going down painfully on unyielding debris. Ignoring the instant hurt he lunged up and around the corner, weapon ready and finger on the trigger. Gratefully, in the illumination of numerous small fires he saw that she was upright and kicking at something on the ground. It wasn't responding.

"What are you doing?"

She turned, a wild grin on her face.

"Taking out the trash."

"Wes! Wes!"

Wes and Juddy were looking over the old Scout, she looked intact, and all the gauges seemed to be functioning as they should. Their paintwork however, had suffered. They couldn't tell that much in the dark. The transmission ended the inspection.

"Yes, old lad."

"Can that thing still fly?"

Wes exchanged a pained expression with Juddy, who'd heard the question. Juddy mouthed, *that thing?*

"Our aircraft, though bruised, appears intact, old lad. Why? Where do you need us?"

James was crouched beside a broken wall, Bailey beside him. The news she'd brought had complicated things. Tyres were popping, shards of automotive glass and metal were airborne and deadly. The houses weren't cleared, there might be gangsters in the undergrowth, Ames was alone in the church with Cela, his own hands were full and as reluctant as he was, he had to agree with Bailey.

"Get back here as quick as you can, pick up Bailey, then get over to Tom and Sacha. We think the estate is being attacked, the five of you have got to get there asp!"

James could hear the turbine being wound up in the background. For big men, those guys knew how and when to move.

"On our way old lad, with the speed of a Tall Indian."

WTF? James let that go, there wasn't time for it and aviators had a language of their own. Bailey ran to a clear space, downrange, away from the fighting. She popped smoke, the fires from the burning cars illuminating it.

The Scout flared in, its skids barely touching before Bailey was aboard and looking to strap in. There were no seats in the rear, just a plain, metal floor with a few fittings here or there. She found a length of green webbing, no wider than an inch or two. She grabbed the hanging headphones.

"It that it?" She shouted above the commotion of the clattering aircraft, holding the woefully inadequate strap up for inspection.

"Operational mode!" Shouted Juddy. "You may also have noted the lack of doors." He smiled evilly. "Tie yourself on and sit outboard, with your feet on the skids. You'll be fine."

"Says you!" she shouted back, "on an armoured, padded seat with a four-point harness!"

They were barely in the air before descending again. On seeing and hearing its approach, Tom and Sacha had packed up their position and were running towards the aircraft. Juddy thumbed them rearwards. The two girls took one skid, Tom the other. The aircraft battered through the night, on course for the estate.

Adey was in his element. Lyla was an interested party, and he was enjoying this rare moment in the sun. She quizzed him on equipment, techniques and was absorbed in the lab, soaking up knowledge. Hearing the alarm and remembering what Sacha had whispered to her before leaving, she ran from the lab and into the office. Looking at the perimeter monitors she could see the intruders, three, at least, and they didn't look at all friendly. Remembering the advice and codes Sacha had given her, she wrenched open the sideboard doors, located the small, steel facia, keyed the code in and opened the gun safe. Checking the contents and not thinking too hard about what they might shortly be forced to do, she grabbed the keys to their survival. From there, she shot back to Adey, told him what was coming and asked if he had any useful formulae. Confused about his role but seeing what she was carrying in her hands, he grasped the deadly nature of their situation, and began rummaging in cupboards. Lyla dashed upstairs.

Snake was enjoying this. Sure, he couldn't understand a word the two guys ahead were saying but that wouldn't spoil the moment. He had a gun in his hand, a gun with bullets in it. It wasn't a Glock 19, just some piece of Czech iron but the Glock would come. He was certain of it now. He crept across the lawns behind them, balletically recreating scenes from the movies, his gun arm sweeping theatrically at imaginary enemies, firing off devastatingly accurate storms of bullets. He was Ninja, bending bullets around corners, and leaving his targets open mouthed at his skill and dexterity. His gut had a warmth that was spreading, he was about pissing himself with excitement and anticipation. *Snake is coming,* he said to himself, *be afraid, I am the assassin, I am death.* He pirouetted once, arms raised, lips pursed. There was an angry hiss from up front. Snake stopped fantasising, embarrassed at being caught. He acknowledged the rebuke while thinking, *don't cross me, man. You'll regret it. I got me a gun.* He looked lovingly down once more, relishing the feel of it, then got with the program. They were through the fence and heading for the house. Someone knew they were coming; the alarm had been silenced and all the lights extinguished but Snake wasn't stressed. Just an old man and a girl, they'd said. No problem.

Peter Christian had a safe room but had decided against using it. The alarm and subsequent arrival of an animated Lyla had startled him. She'd explained that there were three men heading through the grounds. With Adey in the lab and Beatrice in a drug induced coma, there were four of them, too many to fit into the safe room.

"What do we do?" Asked Christian, surprising himself in offering the initiative to his young friend.

"We fight, of course."

"What with, the others aren't here, and those men are certain to be thugs."

Christian recalled the aura of danger exuding from his kidnappers. It would be wise to assume the intruders were of the same ilk.

From the waistband of her jeans Lyla flourished the two pistols Sacha had said were in the gun safe. Placing one on Christian's desk, she held the other up for inspection. Pulling back on the slide, she illustrated that the weapon was empty. Letting the slide go forwards under its spring, she released the tension on the hammer, and produced a magazine, its top shiny with brass. She slipped the mag into the butt, pulled back the slide again making it ready to fire.

"This is the safety catch, when it's in line with the red dot." She tilted the pistol to show the marker. "It's ready to fire. All you have to do is point and pull the trigger. I don't have to tell you there'll be a loud bang and some kickback. Be ready for it. And only point it at the bad guys."

Christian was astonished with the ease and expertise Lyla illustrated when handling such a deadly object. Reluctantly, he took the foreign object from her, hefting it in his hand. He watched her as she repeated the loading process with the second gun then held it easily in her right hand. Feeling like a fraudulent gunfighter, he mimicked her stance then looked at her.

"Lyla. How do you know all this? How to do all this?"

She smiled, remembering all the secret hours in the bunker with Sacha, only Ollie aware of what they were up to.

"My Mom taught me."

Back in the lab, Adey had been busy and creative.

"A bit of Naphtha, some Quicklime, and a touch of phosphorous."

"What will that do?"

"It'll ignite spontaneously on contact with air, I haven't had time to make it potent, and I was working in the dark. It may only burn for a short time. We need to get it on their clothes, skin, or hair."

"How much have you got?"

He looked pained, knocking this stuff up without leading to self-immolation was a precise art.

"Just the one."

"Take it to the first-floor landing. If you get the chance, drop it like a grenade and Adey,"

"Hm?"

"Try not to burn the house down."

The front door had defeated them. Too thick and hardened by age. No matter, a broken window will do as well. Snake crouched behind the two big guys as they smashed their way in. Inside, it was pitch black. They were in an office where a greyer shade of light led into a hallway and they crept silently down, the carpet muffling their progress, Snake crouching, sweeping his gun arm theatrically from side to side. Creaking open a couple of doors revealed no occupants, so they continued their search. To their right, they could make out a staircase leading upwards. Ignoring it in favour of clearing the ground floor first, the three trespassers paused. There was a creak from above, just the slightest sound betraying a presence, it was the last sensible thought they processed. Looking up something fell, tumbling, glistening, then striking Snake square on the forehead, shattering on impact. Globules of fluorescence and heat splashed between the three men, igniting clothing, and creating panic. Then from the darkness ahead, the muzzle flashes and sharp reports of shots being fired straight at them. The confusion was utter, and Snake, his head ablaze, blinded, began pulling his trigger, trying to kill the agony. The big man in front of him dropped, his skull shattered from behind by a Czech bullet. Snake kept pulling until from somewhere, he heard an empty click, then another as his flaming hair was consumed and his scalp began to feel its touch. He couldn't be sure but reckoned he was standing alone, the man to his left having been hit from the front. He dropped his gun, flapping his hands at his head, beating at the flames, but something stuck to his hands and suddenly, everything he touched began to burn. He fell to his knees, his existence unbearable.

As the vial dropped and the fire started, Lyla and Christian, emerged together from the old billiard room. Clearly lit and at this range, they were unmissable. Lyla fired four shots, two each into the body mass of the men closest to her, she could see a third behind, but he was well alight and firing off rounds like he was at a Taliban wedding. A skull erupted but it hadn't been caused by her pistol. She glanced at Christian beside her. He hadn't caused it either. He had his eyes closed and his gun pointing in the general direction of away. She saw the hall chandelier shatter and plaster fall from the ceiling.

The scene settled, the two biggest guys were down, the third was on his knees, the flames had died, and all were smouldering.

Snake was registering stuff. The pain had gone, his nerve endings destroyed. He thought that the lights had come on and that there was someone standing over him. While he recognised that they might be a threat, his mind was wandering, looking for his dream, finding it, he recalled he had a name. Snake. Disappointment registered when the realisation struck that as far as his future was concerned, he would only be called that because he no longer had any ears. Tears were falling, he thought, vaguely, then he heard a voice.

Lyla warily approached the three intruders. Two were out of the game. She could see no rise or fall of the chest and the eyes she could see were wide, dead. She turned her attention to the kneeling man. From the noise he had been making and the havoc his trigger finger had wreaked she reckoned his gun was empty and besides, was on the floor. She kicked it away anyway; she'd seen that on the TV and figured it was the thing to do.

There was a low, keening noise coming from his throat and she could see tears rolling down his cheeks. His arms were limp down his sides. Adey's stuff had done its thing and while it had all been loud, hot, and busy, it was over. An adrenalin rush made her limbs tremble and her stomach rebel, feeling suddenly sick. She bit back, holding it down. From above she heard a voice.

"Everything ok down there?"

"Your stuff worked. Adey." She called back, her voice tight, her throat dry. "You can come down now."

The kneeling man's injuries didn't look fatal, just painful, and ugly, his hands and face peeling and blackened, hair burnt away. She was considering what to do with him when her eye caught something. Something strangely familiar, a thing from her past. Leaning down, looking for confirmation that she could believe what she was seeing, she plucked it from his jacket.

Her tears were instant, clouding her vision but she needed to see, had to know. Her sleeve cleared the worst of them and through the mist, she recognised it for what it was. She gripped the butt of her pistol, flexing her fingers and her mind. She got down, level, face to face with the kneeling man.

"Where did you get this?" Her voice wasn't her own. The stink of the man and her own reaction to events had it emanating from between clenched teeth.

"What?" Snake knew he'd heard a voice, perhaps even been asked a question. He tried to focus. He felt a slap, was sure some skin had slid from his face.

"Where did you get this?"

There was something in front of his eyes. He pulled his head back, it was too far, he zoomed in and saw what it was. He smiled at the memory, burnt, cracked, and blackened lips stretching, splitting. He couldn't feel it.

"A souvenir. I took it."

"From who? Tell me! Who did you take it from?"

The voice had got louder, he reckoned it might even be angry, but the memory made him smile. The knife sliding in. His triumphant return to the trap house, rucksack aloft, like the FA Cup.

“A kid. Just a kid. Knifed him. Me. A good day out. Wassamatter? It’s just a fucking badge?”

Lyla looked harder at the image. The constellation Libra and remembered the day she’d given it to Paul.

“No. It’s not just a fucking badge.”

One handed, she gripped the front of what was left of his jacket and holding him steady, showed him her gun.

“Man,” He smiled, dreamily. “That’s a Glock 19. Always wanted me one o’ them.”

Lyla gave it to him, blowing Snakes brains out, from right to left.

She pushed the corpse away, watched it drop, heard it fall. Walking into the kitchen, she ran the tap, took soap, a brush and scrubbed the small, metal insignia while the tears ran down her face. Sobbing, she found a towel, dried it, then polished it. There was a mirror above the sink and as she pinned the memento, the symbol of a moment in time to her stained shirt, she smiled sadly at herself, and closed her eyes and saw Paul, as he was then. No, not just a badge.

The kitchen door opened and with Adey supporting him, Christian struggled in. His complexion was unnaturally pale, a horrified Lyla saw blood dripping onto the floor.

Grey faced, Christian made it to a chair, slumped and before he fainted said simply, “I believe I may have been shot.”

The helicopter clattered gamely across the countryside, Wes and Juddy grimly keeping it aloft. When the estate hove into view below, Sacha noted dismally that all the lights were out. Then, as they landed and she was running towards the house, a solitary light came on inside. Tom was getting ahead of her, racing up the lawn. She pulled alongside of him; weapon ready as they got to the door. It was locked, impenetrable. With a cry of frustration she ran to the nearest window. Tom boosted her up then followed her in, Bailey right behind him. The smell was awful. Burnt furnishings, flesh, hair, cordite. Smoke hung high up in the hall ceiling and the view that greeted them brought a demented howl from Sacha’s throat. There was blood, blackened corpses, three of them in a pile.

“Lyla! Lyla!”

“In here.” The reply seemed reasoned, relaxed almost, giving Sacha hope. She rushed to the source of the voice, the kitchen, and burst in. Lyla was cutting PC’s shirt away. There was blood everywhere.

“Bailey!”

“Right behind you, Sacha. Let me get my kit.”

Lyla had a hand on PC. Putting pressure on a bloody hole high up on his chest. Sacha waited; hands pressed hard by her sides in frustration. Her girl was doing the right thing, she wouldn't spoil it now. Bailey came back, opened her kit and moving Lyla to one side, began working on the wounded man.

Sacha stood still; arms outstretched as Lyla came towards her. Smoke greased, stinking, covered in sweat-streaked blood, the young girl moved forwards and buried her head. Sacha stroked her hair mumbling nothing but mumbling it softly. When she'd collected herself, she whispered, "The gun safe. You opened it."

Shyly, Lyla pulled away slightly, retrieving the Glock from her waistband and holding it up for Sacha to see.

"Thanks Mum. I know what it is I want to do."

In the church, the Albanian was moving closer, then, in the dark, Ames's phone shattered the stillness.

"Stay where you are Mister Cela, or I shall open fire. I have to take this."

"Of course." Came the Albanians reply, much closer that Ames would have liked. Ames increased the distance between them, adding a discarded pew for comfort. He raised the instrument to his ear and listened.

"Thank you, Tom. No, I think everything is pretty much under control. Any chance of getting the helicopter back?" A pause while he listened again.

"I thought as much. Thank you."

"Something to tell me, Mister Clever Man?"

"That was the estate, your people weren't up to the task."

Ames had been half expecting the attack, but still, it erupted so quickly he barely had chance to raise his gun arm and instinctively fire.

The roar of rage and frustration that had spat from Altin's throat was wasted, halted as it was by the passage of a Winchester Silvertip 9mm parabellum round. With a weight of 7.5 grams and a muzzle velocity of 1,225 feet per second it virtually removed his head from his body. With no instructions from above, the strings cut, his torso folded on top of his limbs, and he went down like a sack of shit, now quite low on the Adonis index.

Ames's hand trembled when he saw what he had done, then as his mind considered the alternative, his ordered intellect settled the matter as a fair and just outcome. The trembling ceased and he began to understand James, Ollie, and the others just a little better and that he wasn't a copper, not anymore. Ollie burst through the door, gun up, scanning. Understanding the scene, he lowered the weapon.

“Alright, Boss.” He enquired softly.

“Fine thank you, Ollie. How are things outside?”

“Just finishing off, Boss.”

“Casualties?”

“Loads of ‘em, Boss. Mostly theirs.”

“Mostly?”

“Dave has taken a hit to his right eye, if you ask me, he’s gonna lose it.”

“Oh. Ok.” *Christ! An eye!* “How is he?”

Ames thought about the price these people paid, mentally, physically, for the choices they made. An eye, potentially gone forever. Did these people consider such injuries an occupational hazard? Then he remembered that they weren’t *these* people, they were *his* people. He couldn’t help himself and closed his right eye, viewing temporarily what might well be Dave’s permanent window on the world.

Ollie saw Ames struggling with the news and reached out gripping Ames’s upper arm.

“Boss, he’s ok. He says there’s no pain. It’s happened, he’ll cope.”

Ames shrugged off his temporary gloom. Coping. That was the answer, apparently. He reopened his eye, beginning to understand how facts of life needed to be faced.

"Fine. Off you pop then, go join your mates, I'll be out directly."

"Gotcha, Boss."

Ollie gave a dirt smeared grin and with a thumbs up gesture, left the church.

Ames strolled out reflectively. He reckoned the sun would be up in about five hours. He had work to do, then he needed to lay his hands on a bottle of scotch and some glasses.

It was while policing the battlefield that the true cost of the operation struck home.

"Anyone seen Sid?"

No-one had. The tidy up was as dangerous as creating the mess. Instant kills were rarer than Hollywood would have you believe, and wounded men were every bit as dangerous as the able bodied, occasionally more so. They were short-handed. Neil was patching Dave up which left just five of them to seek and destroy. It was during the sweep that Sid was found.

“Jesus, Sid.” There was a lot of blood, mostly centre mass. One look told Ollie most of what he needed to know. He unwrapped the tactical keffiyeh covering Sid’s head and beard. The old man blinked, his skin was cool and pale, his breathing rapid, his pulse thready. He didn’t have long. Ollie got down to his knees, carefully rearranging the crumpled Australian into something approaching comfortable, eventually lying beside him, his head in the crook of his arm.

“I know, mate.” The old Australian croaked. “Got two of the bastards,” Sid, breathless, paused to drag in air. “Never saw the third ‘til it was too late. Buggers were sneakin’ round the back.”

There were three bodies nearby. Their large and fatal wounds evidence of the old SLR’s fabled stopping power.

“You got ‘im though.”

Sid nodded, or his head slumped to his chest, Ollie couldn’t tell. He felt the back of Sid’s neck tense, trying to raise his head to make breathing easier. Ollie’s hand gently did the job. Sid smiled, fingers fluttering in a gesture of gratitude. “Yeah. Reckon I did.”

The AK47 punches out a slow, heavy bullet which, beyond 200 yards, is unlikely to hit anything it is aimed at. But Sid had been hit at close range by three of them, he wasn’t getting up again and both he and Ollie knew it.

"This is me done...then."

Ollie looked at the wounds. One in the belly, two more, stitching up and left. He couldn't lie, but facing the truth was equally difficult, he wouldn't disrespect the old soldier with deceit.

"Stands a chance."

Sid's hand waved around, looking for something. Ollie took it in his, feeling a squeeze of thanks in response. They lay together quietly, Sid blinking, looking at the stars, Ollie down at the old man. Sid tried to talk but was struggling, individual words intruding staccato while he battled for air.

"The...others?"

"A few scratches, nothing more."

"Not...my day...then."

"Seems not."

A smile flitted across the old man's face.

"Well...when you...gotta go...you..."

A terminal cough finished the sentence and with it, Sid. Ollie cradled the old man, a man he'd known since that first day at the 'kill house', where Sid had been his instructor. Even then, all those years ago, he'd seemed ancient, at least by SF standards. His death would reverberate around the community. Another one that hadn't beaten the clock. It had been a long time since Ollie had wept. But he did it now.

SID

"Who knew?" James and Ollie were going through Sid's personals. There was nothing remarkable until the discovery of a small, carved camphorwood chest. Inside was a rack of medals, five in all, apparently foreign, definitely not British.

"This one's got a bar on the ribbon. Says Vietnam."

"Bugger me," Ollie breathed, producing a black and white, dog-eared photo. "Look at this."

It was of a very young Sid. In jungle fatigues and a slouch hat.

"Who knew?" Ollie repeated. "He never said."

"The Aussies were there from'62 to'75." James recollected. "It was his era, or at least part of it."

"What do we do with 'em."

"Not just them, these." James produced another, more familiar rack.

There was a Distinguished Conduct Medal, The Military Medal, a General Service Medal with three clasps, Dhofar, Lebanon and Northern Ireland with an oak leaf on the ribbon, denoting a

Mention in Dispatches, a Falklands medal with rosette denoting combat and a Long Service and Good Conduct Medal.

"If they could talk. Looks like he was busy for nearly 30 years."

"Did you ever see him in dress uniform?"

"I'd remember if I had, with that lot on he'd have had a bit of the Idi Amin about him."

"Point taken. What do we do with them?"

James thought about that. Sid had left a simple will, that all his worldly goods should go to the Sanctuary with one simple request attached. That there should always be a stray named Sid, in keeping with his own lifestyle. He'd stated no living relatives or desire to be sent home, if they could make it happen, he'd like to stay here.

"We'll buy them, hand the cash over then get them cased along with that photo. Can't see any point in burying them with him and it'll be a reminder of who he was and what we didn't know."

"Works for me." Replied Ollie. "Shall we go and have a word? I'd like them to know."

Sid's photos and medals were laid out on the kitchen table.

"He was seventy-seven last birthday."

"Who was he, exactly?"

Ollie stroked the ribbons before replying. "My first OC, as it happens."

Sacha's eyebrows lifted. "An officer, that long haired surfer dude was an officer?"

"A major, to be precise."

"Fuck me. That explains a lot." Tom recalled the boys clear respect and deference when around the old man.

"From the look of this lot, the bars on the GSM, he must have come to us after Vietnam. I heard stories in the Mess. Sid never gave orders, just suggested a course of action, that way, if it all went tits up, and initiative was needed, no-one could be accused of disobeying a direct order. Very Australian. Neat. He must have got those two," Ollie pointed to the MM and DCM, "before he was commissioned, otherwise it would have been an MC and a DSO."

"Rose through the ranks, then."

"Yep." Said Ollie. "I loved that old man."

"And you, James." Asked Sacha. "How well did you know him?"

"Same as Ollie, pretty much." James wasn't going to be drawn. He had his own memories.

"I know a bit about these." Tom picked up the Vietnam rack.

"How?" Ollie asked, his interest piqued, the Vietnam medals had been a surprise, he thought he'd known the old man..

Tom wanted to get this right. It was obvious the boys knew nothing, which he now thought a little odd. Thinking, he decided that the only way to tell it was how it happened.

"It was last summer."

Sacha and the girls were on a night out, leaving Tom twiddling his thumbs. There was nothing on the TV, he didn't fancy a book. In an effort to get some air in the house, Tom had opened all the windows and the glass patio doors that led to the lawns. It made little difference and though in shorts and a T shirt, Tom was sweaty and uncomfortable. The cooler air outside offered some respite so, he decided that a stroll couldn't hurt. His attention was instantly drawn to the summer house, Sid's bolthole. An outside light was on. He could hear music and saw Sid, feet up, on the veranda, a big old dog stretched out full length on the deck and a pedestal fan powering in an arc from left to right, delivering relief from the oppressive, still milieu. The old Aussie made a beckoning motion and grateful for the distraction, Tom wandered over.

Sid had a hand rolled cigarette on the go, an old Dansette with a stack of vinyl playing gamely and a bottle of Jack.

"Park yerself, mate. Drink? Glasses are in the sink."

"Madness not to." Replied Tom, retrieving a short glass from the kitchenette and pulling a chair up.

"Smoke?"

"I'm on a ban."

"Got a spare rolled. It's just there, mate."

Sacha knew that Tom enjoyed the occasional smoke. It was probably the only bone of contention between them. Tom had 'quit', years back but the tug was still there, and Sacha was out. Tom took the spare.

"Got a light?"

Sid produced a battered old zippo, flicked the lid and friction wheel in a single movement and sparked Tom up.

He eased back in the chair, and ignoring the foul but anticipated taste, took in a deeply satisfying lungful. Lifting the glass, he raised it in a toast.

"Cheers, Sid.

"No worries. Missus not around then?"

"Out with the girls."

Sid waved his cigarette. "That explains your courage."

"Nasty old bastard, never liked you."

Sid chuckled at the oft repeated remark, it underwrote the easy relationship both men shared. They sat quietly, listening to the night and the scratchy old record player. Casting around, Tom's gaze fell on the old zippo. Something he'd never seen or perhaps not noticed before. Sid kept his cigarette habit to his own environs.

Tom noticed it was brass, battered but engraved. He picked it up and studied it. It was crested and though worn by use; he could just make out the details. At the centre, a kangaroo with crossed rifles behind. Beneath it, an inscribed boomerang, the letters too worn to make out. The whole thing was surrounded by a laurel wreath or similar and surmounted by a crown.

"What's the story?"

Sid reached out for the lighter. "This old thing?" He paused for perhaps a minute or two, which in a silence between two men, when a question has been asked, feels like forever. Reaching some kind of inner settlement, Sid rolled a ciggy, lit it, then handed the makings and the lighter to Tom.

"The bit you can't read says '6th Battalion Royal Australian Regiment'."

Tom waited, understanding the pause that sometimes naturally comes between information and a story.

"I was a Nasho."

"Eh?"

"National serviceman, a conscript. It started in '64, can't say when it finished. Like winning at bingo. The Birthday Ballot, they called it. Twice a year, the bastards up top pulled a date out of a hat. If you were one of the lucky ones you got to do two years regular, three years reserve. It made for some epic, mass birthday parties on base."

Sid took a pull from his glass of Jack and a lungful of smoke, then leaned back and reminisced.

"It was 1966, I was twenty or thereabouts. Us Aussies and the Kiwis got ourselves involved; don't ask me how, I didn't ask, in Vietnam."

This got Tom's interest. He'd been vaguely aware that this had been the case but had never really looked into it.

"We were all conscripts, well, mostly. A couple of officers and NCOs had done Malaya but the rest of us were fresh out of the box."

Sid took a drag from his cigarette, then blew smoke rings.

"Long Tan." Two words spoken at length.

"August it was. Bloody weather was kak. Anyway, buggers mortared our base one night. Killed one, wounded a few so the Gods on high reckoned we should wander outside the wire and poke a few bears. Trouble was, Int was a crock. Thought we were up against maybe thirty of forty of the bastards, turned out it was nearer 2,500."

Tom's eyebrows shot up a notch as the numbers were crunched.

"Long and the short of it is the next day out in the boonies, one of our platoons got isolated, mostly wiped out as it happens. The rest of us spent most of our time trying to get to 'em, which eventually, we did. 108 of us when we started. Sixty-nine left standing when it was all over. We lost eighteen dead, twenty-one wounded. Artillery saved us, I reckon. Check it out, it's on Wiki."

Tom didn't know how to acknowledge this rare insight, so taking Sid's cue, thought long before responding.

"After that?"

Sid sat up and stubbed out his fag.

"There's another bit you can't read." Sid picked up the zippo and pointed out a small inscription below the kangaroo's feet.

"Duty First, it says. It's a good motto for anybody. So I did my five years then decided to check out the Old Country. Not much in the way of family left in Oz so I ended up staying. Got pissed one night, enlisted the next day. Can't even remember when that was."

"That's it?"

"As far as I can remember, the night got a bit shabby after a while. There was the usual Australia'll kill you banter, you know, Red Back, Mouse Spider, Wolf Spider, Black House Spider, Funnel Web. *'And that's just the stuff that lives in the house.'"* Tom mimicked, in classic Sid. "Between us we finished the Jack."

"You were smoking?" Sacha was frowning.

"That's what you got from that?" Tom chided; fairly certain the accusation would be incoming. Sacha was just about to fire something back when James stepped in.

"He needs to be laid to rest our way. There'll be a few people turn up."

The decision to bury Sid in the grounds had complications but he hadn't specified a location and they wanted to keep him close.

"If it's not a problem for you, then it isn't for us." Offered Tom.

"Leave space either side." Said Ollie. "I've got nowhere else to go. Where are the shovels?"

Sid's Australian Blue Ensign flew at half-mast, snapping in the freshening breeze. The wreath was of dark and light blue coloured flowers. The word had gone out and men as old as eighty stood beside the fresh grave. In keeping with tradition, berets removed during the service were replaced as the last post was played. Then Ollie delivered the final words over their fallen comrade.

"We are the Pilgrims, Master we shall go always a little further, it may be beyond that last blue mountain barred with snow across that angry or that glimmering sea."

It was important that Sid's last resting place was known, another tradition being that the site would be visited at least once every five years and a fresh wreath laid. People, these people, had to know where he was. Bailey had issued the death certificate and glossed over the cause of death, Sid was of an age, after all. No-one asked why his plot was here, at Tom and Sacha's, adjacent to a small copse given over to a pet cemetery. There were worse places to be, they knew. Later, they held the wake at the summer house, where there were introductions, lamp swinging, extravagant claims, and fond if unreliable memories of old soldiers.

Sacha saw James and Ollie deep in conversation with a huge, bald, black dude. With an eye for detail, Sacha noted that he seemed not to own a jacket and though pressed and polished, his shirt and shoes had seen better days. His regimental tie was precisely knotted, his top collar button done up. She wandered over, intrigued.

"Hi, guys."

James went through the formalities.

"Sacha, meet Noah."

A massive, meaty hand enveloped her own. The palm was calloused, he was missing a finger. She noted the frayed cuff of his shirt. "Missus Hood, glad to meetya."

"Likewise."

She recognised the accent. "Fiji? Samoa?"

"Fiji, missus. Not been back in a while though."

James took Sacha to one side. "He walked here."

"What?" Their home was some distance off the beaten track.

"Where from?"

"He didn't say, took him a day or so though. Got cleaned up in town before making an appearance."

"You're saying all he has he's standing up in?"

"Pretty much. Can he crash here tonight? Me 'n Ollie'll sort him out in the morning. He's not a charity case, but a hand up wouldn't hurt."

Sacha didn't think twice. The man had a calmness to him, a zen like quality that steadied.

"Whatever he needs."

The following day, not wishing to intrude on the long-held traditions of the Regiment, they held their own, personal memorial service, the gathering consisting of everyone from the big house, the ladies from the sanctuary, Sacha, Tom, and Lyla. A little later, after the house had emptied and the afternoon sun was fading, Sacha approached Tom.

"Honey?"

"Hm?" Tom had been sat, quietly working his way through the crossword.

"It's Inga. She wants to…"

Tom stood, folded his newspaper and taking his wife's hand, led them outside. In the middle distance, they could see Inga, robed and standing by Sid's grave.

"Come on, then. Let's see him off."

This was unexpected and Sacha held him back. "You're ok with this?"

Tom recalled a long-ago conversation with his old friend and smiled.

"What's life without a bit of magic in it?"

SINTON-LAMONT

The call came from Estate Security interrupting what until now, eclipsed by the loss of Sid, had been a delightful evening. James had flogged his guts out transforming the old billiard room into a stylish mix of contemporary and traditional and had managed it just in time for Lyla's eighteenth birthday celebration. As it turned out, he had an ulterior motive, an announcement of his own.

"Millie's pregnant." There was a moment of open-mouthed surprise broken by Ollie.

"What does that mean?"

"It means we're going to have a baby, numbnuts." Millie replied, her huge smile a match for James's.

There was the usual, *'You ok? When's it due? Is it a boy or a girl?'* Fended off with *'Fine. August. Don't know, don't wanna know.'*

Once the shock of that had worn off and a toast drunk, Lyla sought Sacha out.

"Not you as well?" Sacha teased.

"No! Of course not! How would I?" Seeing Sacha's grin, Lyla gave her a friendly punch on the shoulder and a statement.

“I want to do a Criminology degree.”

Sacha knew there was more to this than just further education. Despite the warmth of their community, Sacha was aware that Lyla felt isolated, separated from her own generation. She wanted to mix, meet, and engage with others of a similar age to her own. It was inevitable and therefore not unexpected. Sacha and Tom though, were wary.

“It’s her choice to make.” Sacha had said.

“I know.” Agreed Tom. “But there’s a lot to think about, what happens if she lets something slip?”

“What do we do, Tom? Keep her locked up?”

Both knew that wasn’t an option, but some hard discussions would need to be had. The first would be about the name change they felt was necessary.

Sacha let the memory of that conversation slide as she scanned the room.

“Let’s walk and talk.”

They’d made the decision that the ladies could not be left out of this so under the guise of Christian being an uncle, they’d been invited to the party. Listening, strolling with Lyla, Sacha was distracted, entertained by the dynamic in the room. Inga had Adey cornered, witchcraft meeting science. Superficial contradictions that apparently, were not mutually exclusive, simply the accumulation of data through observation and experiment. That one was going to run and run, she thought, as Adey struggled with Inga's argument that science was limited, while magic was not. Donna and Neil were deep in conversation about why cars should or shouldn't have names or send and receive Christmas cards while Yvette was inspecting Dave's eye patch. PC, his arm in a sling, was chatting with Ames who was himself, patched up, stitches on a long cut just beneath his hairline. The discussion was based around the kidnap.

"You either get a mobile phone or I'm going to have a tracker injected into your neck." Christian winced, Sacha sensed an agreement would be reached soon.

James and Millie were in a corner, deep in conversation. Millie was aware that James had an unusual occupation and Sacha wondered if the chat was about whether that should change. Millie had scanned the room, pointing at the walking wounded, James appeared to be struggling with an explanation. Sacha was uncertain how that would end.

Scott and Jules were engaged in a jocular debrief with Wes and Juddy.

"Mad bitch." Scott declared, quietly. "Some days I feel like a passenger on the Meltdown Express. You know she set fire to her folks' home when she was a kid. They found her in an Ottoman chewing on a bacon sandwich."

Jules jabbed him with an elbow. "Bad dog, no biscuits." They were laughing. "And on that subject, I'm peckish. Ollie!" she shouted. "Have you got cheesy wotsits behind that bar?"

Ollie grinned, noting the opening. "I don't know you well enough to say!"

Jules gave him the finger and returned to Scott's monologue, who, undeterred by the interruption, was in full flow. "We had to go to a wedding once. Guess who stopped en route to pick up flowers to decorate the car?"

"Nothing wrong with that."

"Agreed, Juddy, except she stopped at a graveyard and made her selection there."

"Point taken."

But there was no stopping Scott. "So, I'd lost her around a corner, heard shooting, went over on my arse and by the time I got up again, I was pretty much ready for anything, a bit tense, you get the picture. Anyway, eventually I get eyes on and there she was, covered in dust, shit, sweat, you name it; a smoking gun in her hand with a massive smile on her face like some heavily armed, demented Cruella De Vil, standing over three of 'em. Dead as doornails, giving one of the stiffs a kick, screaming something like, ‘I bet you wish you were back in Kansas now!’”

“I always wanted to say that. My favourite movie.”

Wes chuckled. “Really? Oddly enough I had Full Metal Jacket in my head.”

“Funny you should mention movies. We were Jason Statham’s security detail on a film shoot. One night, we’re in a bar, she finds an orange box from somewhere and she’s standing on it, meeting him eye to eye, so to speak, delivering a lecture on what he can and can’t do unless she says so, when some drunken arsehole who’d been trying to pick a fight with Jason all night came from nowhere with a broken bottle in his hand. She nutted him over Jason’s shoulder, laid him spark out then carried on chatting to Jace as if nothing had happened.”

“Evening, Ollie, Noah.” Sacha had found them at the end of the bar. At Tom and Sacha’s invitation and with a thumbs up from James and Ollie, Noah had taken up Sid’s role and residence. It had seemed a shame to leave the place empty and Noah had a need and was a good fit.

He smiled broadly. “Lo Missus.” She couldn’t get him to use her name and rather than fight it, decided to like it instead. She smiled back.

Ollie's thumbs were beeping busily on his mobile keyboard. "Ex-wife?"

"Bloody dating apps." He grinned. "I don't chase women but can't always be bothered to run away. I'm supposed to be on a break."

Sacha smiled. "Nor should you. And think what they're missing." She whispered in his ear.

"How about Jimbob 'n Millie? It's gonna change things, isn't it?"

"Didn't I read somewhere that it's the only certain thing in life? Change?"

"I s'pose." Mumbled Ollie, thoughtfully. "But don't think for a minute that I'm gonna turn into some kind of responsible adult. Not happening."

"You'll be fine."

The insistent ring of the telephone was a distraction, so Ollie set aside the conversation to deal with it.

"Guys!" He shouted, from the bar, but went largely unheard. He'd need to get louder. "Guys!"

Ames turned; a drink held loosely in one hand. Having at least gained the attention of one, Ollie beckoned him over.

"What?"

"It's the front gate. There a suit in a limo, got two goons with him. He wants to talk to you."

"He asked for me by name?"

Ollie nodded, raising both eyebrows, and handing the receiver to Ames. There was a brief conversation, mostly one sided with Ames doing the bulk of the listening. Ames replaced the handset slowly, aware that curiosity had overcome the remainder of the room after Ollie had wandered over and explained the somewhat unusual nature of the call. They'd quietly listened to Ames saying little but his expression talking loud and clear. Sacha and Lyla set aside the discussion about her future.

"Boss?" Asked James.

Ames placed his drink on the bar. "We have an uninvited and most likely unwelcome guest. I have no idea where this is going. We don't have a choice about whether to welcome him in, or not. Be very, very careful what you say, or do. Can you ask those three," he indicated Dave, Neil, and Adey, "to distract our guests elsewhere. I have a feeling they shouldn't hear this."

Leaving the room with that cryptic remark Ames headed for the foyer, then outside, as something large, black, and ministerial hove into view, its tyres crunching on the gravel. The rear occupant waited for his door to be opened by a trouser suited, female minion, then unfolded himself from the back of the car. Georgian elegant in a tailored fit, below the knee black overcoat and carrying a furled umbrella, he was tall, lean, with neat cropped white hair that glowed beneath the exterior lighting. He waited for the door to be closed behind him before stepping forwards and introducing himself with an outstretched hand.

"Benedict Sinton-Lamont."

Ames took the hand as a matter of courtesy. He'd heard of BSL and was unhappy at being this up close and personal with Whitehall's hatchet man. It didn't take much deduction to work out why he was here. The man moved underground, flushing government sewage, always involved, rarely named. Perhaps they'd been naïve to think that Themis could remain undiscovered and if Sinton-Lamont was here, using Ames's name as his calling card, it was clear they'd been unearthed. Sinton-Lamont had a look on his face that Ames well recognised. It was Jungle Book, Ka the snake, predatory.

"Shall we go in? I understand we're celebrating."

The words were delivered in crisp, military fashion. Friendly enough but with an undercurrent of deep knowledge and satisfaction.

Silently, Ames gestured towards the entrance, then led, feeling like he was about to be attacked from behind. Ames was off balance and needed time to organise his head. The fact that Sinton-Lamont was here not with a small army or police force, suggested that this wasn't an official visit, that there was room for manoeuvre. Ames believed they were in trouble but what form that trouble would take was yet to be revealed.

Background music could be heard as they approached the bar. Ames felt that that was good, that for the moment, the guys were keeping their powder dry and not treating the interruption with the usual fanfare and terror Sinton-Lamont's presence demanded. Ignorance is bliss, he noted mentally.

Sinton-Lamont took over the instant he entered the room.

"Good evening, everybody. So sorry to disturb your celebrations." The apparent afterthought delivered next cleaved the room. "It's just so difficult to get you all together at the same time. It felt like too good an opportunity to resist."

Behind him, Ames delivered the introduction.

"Guys. Meet Benedict Sinton-Lamont. His job description is vague."

Sinton-Lamont turned, smiling at Ames. "Would you mind, Stuart, joining your friends. I find it awkward when my attention is split."

Ames retrieved his drink from the bar and did as asked. They were grouped in a loose semi-circle, Sinton-Lamont at its base.

"Hi, Ruby." Bailey had directed the greeting at Lamont-Sinton's aide. "I wasn't expecting to see you any time soon."

"Bailey." And an inclination of the head and a slight smile was the not unpleasant acknowledgement.

"Well," Lamont-Sinton clasped his hands together as a teacher might. "Here we all are. You know my name, Ruby here clearly has a friend in the room and of course, I know who you are. Shall we have a drink and a chat?"

A firm believer that action was preferable to inaction, Ollie strolled behind the bar. "BSL? Sounds like a Korean boy band. What's your poison?"

Sinton-Lamont gave him a mock frown and pursed lips.

"Oliver, isn't it? Unless I miss my guess, the more feral of the Jones Boys." He paused for effect, Ollie hadn't flinched, so BSL continued. "I'll take a scotch, single malt if you have it?"

Smiling, Ollie removed a half empty bottle from a tantalus. The beige label featured pop art beneath a bronzed headline, 'The Macallan'.

Sinton-Lamont's eyebrows notched up, then notched up again. He asked for, and was given the bottle, rolling it in his hands.

"The Macallan 1926. With Valerio Adami artwork. One sold recently at Sotheby's; £2.1million, I understand."

Christian stepped up. "Not this one." Coffee and Malts were his passion.

“Clearly, you know your whisky. So, you are probably aware that there were only ever forty bottles of this produced, two of which have disappeared. The one Oliver is holding was believed to have been destroyed in the Sendai earthquake of 2011, not so, as you can see. The other, unlabelled bottle is in my study, upstairs.”

“May I?” Enquired Sinton-Lamont, fully aware of the legendary status afforded this vintage.

“Of course. What is it if it isn’t tasted?”

Ollie produced a glass and held it up to the light. “If I haven’t wiped this, I’ve at least licked it clean.”

Sinton-Lamont ignored the remark as he watched the precious amber being poured into a fine, pristine, crystal glass. “Lemonade with that?” Ollie asked, innocently, before handing the drink across the bar.

“That’s very kind but thank you, no.” Sinton-Lamont swirled the malt, nosed it, repeated the process twice more, then sipped, giving the appearance of chewing the liquid. That done, he drew in a breath of air, savouring the taste and the moment.

“My compliments, Mister Christian. It must have taken some courage to uncork that bottle.”

Christian shrugged. "Imagine, for a moment, Mister Sinton-Lamont, that it had been destroyed in the earthquake, what would have been the point of it then?"

Sinton-Lamont sipped quietly, knowing that this was a unique experience, never to be repeated and if spoken of, disbelieved.

"Thank you. And now that you've softened me up, the real reason I'm here."

No-one believed that Sinton-Lamont had been softened up. Impressed maybe, but soft? Not in a million years.

He nodded towards Tom and Sacha. "Mister and Mrs. Hood. I have no problem whatsoever with your very understandable reaction to the death of your daughter, Ellen. You have my deepest sympathy and some admiration. Whatever comes from tonight's tete a tete, rest assured that as far as I'm concerned, there are nor will there ever be any repercussions." He paused, giving no explanation for the source of his information nor indeed, why it was any concern of his. He was simply saying that he knew what they had done without implying any threat.

"However, since then, as a group, you've been exceptionally busy. Let me see, the rendition of some British Nationals, from an aircraft at height I believe, over foreign airspace. I can only assume you believe waterboarding too primitive a process or didn't have access to a bucket or two of water and a plank, on the other hand access to an executive jet was no problem,"

He paused mid-narrative, "that said I must offer up a 'very well done'. One supposes that your disinclined freefall display team will not be returning to our shores or appealing to the human rights lobby. How splendidly Machiavellian."

The group remained silent. It was clear there was more coming, so it proved.

"Then there's the small matter of the poisoning of our middle classes which tested Mister Bazalgette and the Metropolitan Board of Works contingency plans regarding the effectiveness of our sewage system and, in the process, amply illustrated the scale of the drug problem facing this country, if not our planet. In mitigation, large numbers of former stakeholders are abstaining, for how long would be speculating. Not too long I hope. Getting anything done at Whitehall is proving impossible, at the moment. Absenteeism is rampant. Apparently, some kind of 'tummy bug.'" Lamont-Sinton paused, mid-flow, studying the diminishing contents of his glass.

"I wonder if you truly considered the ramifications of your, shall we say, 'experiment?'" He began counting on his fingers.

"One imagines GDP will take a hit when the next figures are produced, a blip, of course. Parliament isn't sitting, or if it is, it's in the privacy, or privy, of their own homes. The financial markets are unusually inactive, no brokers, by all accounts. The courts have ground to a halt, lawyers absent. Telephones aren't being answered, post undelivered, television presenters laid low, newspapers lacking columnists and reporters, laboratories without scientists, lay by's decorated with discarded underwear. There's virtually no public transport or taxi's available, most of it undergoing a deep clean. Short of delivering an EMP I find it hard to imagine a more effective way of grinding our fine nation to a halt. I'm told that by Wednesday all should return to normal." He paused again. "You've caused something of a stink." Then smiled at his own joke before continuing,

"I take it no-one here was affected?"

Receiving silence as a response, Lamont-Sinton continued. "Then of course, there's the very recent, fatality heavy incident near Warminster which, given the presence of a quantity of cocaine, is officially listed as a drugs transaction gone awry. That said, I'm told that pyrotechnically, someone amongst you has a career in arranging New Years Eve celebrations. The local population remarking 'how realistic' it all seemed to be compared to HMG's pathetic attempts at laying on a mock battle. I really must have a chat with your armourer chappie."

Ames had been interested to know just how much BSL had learned. The answer was, pretty much everything. There's always someone with better kit and more resources, he considered, ruefully.

But there had to be more to this visit than met the eye. There always was where BSL was concerned. In the distance, he heard him finish recounting their long list of activities.

"Now I have huge admiration for your imaginative use of resources but, that doth butter no parsnips and as a representative of His Majesties Government, I'm rather forced to take a dim view of their buccaneering nature."

Ames stated what he believed to be the obvious. "But you're not here to clap us in irons are you?"

There was a pause before BSL delivered the coup de grace.

"Well, that would be entirely up to you."

Sinton-Lamont let the statement hang in the air briefly, then continued.

"I'm here to make you an offer."

"Didn't I see this once, in The Godfather?" Asked Ollie.

Sinton-Lamont smiled at the reference. "Quite." Then continued. "From time to time, HMG, well, me, specifically, has need of deniable assets. There is also the law of unintended consequences, which in this instance has worked in your favour."

BSL paused, asking for and receiving another malt. His tone was entirely conversational.

"Bujar Cela made an unaccustomed error, grief one supposes, though one can't discount the distinct possibility that an attempt at resurrecting his deceased brother's UK drugs operation was foremost, but that's just the cynic in me. In any event, he journeyed here, very much under the radar. Now our Mr. Bujar was once a principal with the Kosovan Liberation Army and responsible for some particularly nasty war crimes and as such was a person of some interest. The loss of his operation or brother, depending on your faith in human nature, diminished his natural caution for international travel, which was temporarily set aside. The Hague has him now, we delivered him this morning. The free world is falling in love with us again." He raised his glass. "Your country thanks you."

He addressed Christian. "You, sir. Made an astute gamble on the Tirana Stock Exchange."

"It wasn't a gamble. There was a significant sum that one way or another would have found its way into the Albanian economy. I simply wagered on it not arriving."

Another salute with the glass.

"Ladies and Gentlemen, I am no blackmailer, nor do I intend to seek prosecution. You may, if you wish, simply walk away from my partnership proposal, which, if it is to work successfully, needs to be built on trust rather than coercion. I am a patriot and a realist in equal measure." Sinton-Lamont sipped thoughtfully at the diminishing malt.

"Now each and every one of you has an interest in not seeing your activities come to light. You're self-funded, hence no trail to us, or rather, me. You're extremely resourceful and very effective. To paraphrase the youth of today, what's not to like?"

"What do we get in return?"

"My umbrella."

"What's he offering?"

Ames and BSL had disappeared into a back room, emerging an hour or so later. He'd stayed until the last of the 1926 Macallan had been consumed and saluted then faded quietly from the estate. The ladies had been taxied home and the group, Lyla included, were gathered in the billiard room.

"It's odd." Ames was rubbing his temples, trying to make sense of his conversation with BSL. It seemed clear enough, but he was trying to reach through the narrative to discover the motive. In the end, he decided to lay it out and see what the group could come up with.

"He's offering us a cloak, of sorts. We carry on doing what we're doing, he's reasonably content to clear up whatever mess we make but, in the process, he takes the credit for the results. It seems he likes the idea of giving the impression that he has a 'shadow' organisation in his arsenal."

"Define, clear up the mess." James asked, dubious at anything suggested from Whitehall.

"Well, take the Witch Queen upstairs."

"What about her?"

"She's leaving tomorrow morning. Apparently, there is a government run institution where 'difficult' cases are housed, held, call it what you like. It's permanent and off the books. I don't know what to think about that. He mentioned that she might be found one morning on the floor of her kitchen eaten by her own cats."

"I'm sure he was joking."

"I'm not so certain."

James shrugged. Beatrice Hutchison was extremely low down on his list of priorities.

"And we're not expected to give anything in return?"

"Apparently not."

"I don't believe it."

"Neither do I."

UP NEXT

"Ok. It's just us now." They were back home, coffee in hand and sitting at the kitchen table. Sacha was picking up the threads of the interrupted discussion. "You said you wanted to do a Criminology Degree?"

"Yvette says I can get the grades."

Lyla was aware of how difficult this conversation could get. As much as life with Tom and Sacha was full, it was incomplete. Having got over the novelty of the way things are compared to the way things were, she's had a chance to analyse, to think and now felt a sense of isolation. The good things in life, she now realised, were not everything. She craved the company of her peers but knew that this carried risks. Not just to her, but to Sacha and Tom.

Sacha leant across the table, believing she knew where this was going. She was uncomfortable with what must come but understood its inevitability.

"I've thought about it and I want to study criminology."

Well that's something. At least Lyla wasn't asking for a gap year, to travel or whatever it was youngsters did these days.

"Ok." She concurred. "Why?"

Sacha knew from experience that ideals and desires had a nasty habit of changing. This girl had already lost a good deal of her life through no fault of her own. The last thing she needed now was to fritter away her best years on a whim. Sacha needed to understand her motivation and how strong the desire was.

"It's you guys."

"Really? What about us?"

Lyla chose her next words carefully. Her speech was ready in her mind but if it tumbled out instead of rolling, she'd be thought less of.

"Themis. All of it. The stuff you do."

"Keep going."

"Well, look at Adey. That stuff he mixed together made a difference to how things turned out. Education did that. The others, they've learnt how to do stuff that makes a difference, you, and Tom, the same."

Sacha thought this over. In truth, there was nowhere else for Lyla to go. She'd seen too much and experienced too much to ever consider a life outside the organisation.

"And you think a criminology degree is the way to go?"

"I've seen how teamwork functions, thought about what each brings to the party."

"Didn't PC offer to coach you in finance?"

"He did, and I'm grateful, I might even take him up on it but first I need to understand what makes people do the things they do. I want to make a difference."

Sacha made an on-the-spot decision. "Let me show you something."

Standing, she pushed the kitchen table to one side then, searching with her fingertips, found the concealed catch. Flicking it, she lifted a section of floor.

Looking on in surprise, Lyla watched as Sacha hit a switch hidden behind the breakfast bar, the space beneath the trapdoor instantly illuminated. Inclining her head, Sacha indicated that Lyla descend.

She saw a narrow, primitive, timber staircase and as bid, though confused, went down, sensing Sacha right behind her.

The basement was as Tom had left it. Photographs, maps and newspaper cuttings decorating the wall, office paraphernalia strewn across the desk.

Beckoning Lya to take the solitary chair, Sacha sat on the edge of the desk, waiting for the inevitable questions.

"What is this place?" Lyla, glancing around, judged that on the other side of the wall behind her was where all the gardening implements were hung or stored. The remainder of the basement as she'd known it populated by recreational gear. Canoes, summer furniture, it was where she kept her bicycle. She'd had no idea this subterranean extension existed.

"What does it look like?"

Lyla thought briefly and said the first thing that came into her head. "An office?"

"Look at the wall, the pictures."

Lyla took some time. Standing for a closer look, then saw the common denominator.

"It's an operations room."

"This, Lyla, is where it all started for Tom. He built this with his bare hands."

Sacha told the story. Of Tom's solo effort to track and deal with his daughter's murderers. Of his successes, failures, demons. Of the sunny afternoon in a pub garden where her faith had been restored.

"Why are you showing me this, telling me this?"

"You want to do a criminology degree. I figure the best grounding for that has to be to understand cause and effect, the lengths people will go to, how sometimes grit and determination can affect outcomes. Also, I want you to understand Tom. There's more to him than meets the eye. And if the last few weeks has taught you nothing else, you've learned a thing or two about teamwork."

"That's why I want this degree. I don't want to be just a number. I want to contribute, be listened to."

"I know." Said Sacha, simply. "Education, without it you're just a tool, with it, you can become an instrument. So go get your degree."

Back up in the kitchen, the floor restored, Sacha noted a grim set to Lyla's face.

"What am I seeing?"

"I don't know." Lyla confessed. "But I feel sad."

"About?"

"Loneliness, I guess. Living alone in this big house but having your secrets underneath it."

"It was his place. Where he came to fight."

"I'm getting that. Is that why he doesn't like me much? Because I'm here and Ellen isn't?"

Sacha smiled at that. "Is that what you think? You think Tom doesn't like you? Oh, honey, our next conversation is going to blow you away."

Lyla nodded, lately, though Tom had thawed a little, she remained confused by Tom's reticence and aloof manner.

"Trust me, honey. It's not about like or dislike. Tom needed to see where you were going, where we're going and if it's gonna be together. Tom's given a lot to be where we are now. Whatever he has left to give, he 'aint gonna waste it. So he held off. 'til he knew."

Lyla began to see through the cracks, saw some light. That this was about the past, the present and the future. About an investment, not of money, but of emotion, and a little bit of it was about letting go.

"How do you feel about changing your name?"

"What?"

"Tom 'n me. We think we need to lose our surname. We'd like you to join the party."

"Why?"

"Why change it or why bring you into it?"

"Well, both."

Sacha sighed. They'd thought long and hard about this. Both feeling that they'd lose a bit of Ellen but gain privacy, a level of anonymity, the names Tom and Sacha Hood still raised eyebrows, questions. So she laid it out.

"There's that and we think that there's no going back for any of us, you included. What do you think?"

It almost broke Lyla and for a while, speech was impossible. When the tears dried and the words came, they were a simple and heartfelt *'Thank You.'* Lyla Dawson had come and gone, and she would not regret her passing. "What name were you thinking?"

"Mine before I married Tom, Stewart."

Sacha Stewart, Tom Stewart, Lyla Stewart. It hurt to think about that level of belonging. They discussed the legal aspects, none of which were an issue, Bailey had already assured Tom and Sacha that the paperwork was a cinch, but they'd politely declined the offer, this thing would be done right, through all the proper channels. Having given the girl enough to think about for now, Sacha revisited the initial conversation.

"Tell me about the degree."

Sacha wanted to know just how much effort Lyla had put into this idea, to see how serious she was.

"Ok. Let's face it I'm never gonna need an actual job." Lyla indicated her surroundings. "So I've no grand ideas about being a professor or anything like that. I just want to learn about what makes people do the things they do. Pretending now that I understand the curriculum aint gonna fly but Yvette gets me and has given me some pointers. The course I want to do is called Cognitive Forensic Sciences."

"Just the title is over my head, what does it actually teach you?"

"If I knew for sure, I wouldn't be asking you to help me choose."

Lyla paused. This was where it could all go horribly wrong.

"Yvette's been teaching me Italian. I'm getting quite good. Diventari Bravi."

"What?"

"Getting good, like I said. But anyway, the course itself is in English."

Sacha frowned, not in confusion but in gradual realisation.

"Why would that matter? Just where is this course?"

"Rome."

Authors Notes

In this novel, we relied heavily on Themis compromising the Encrochat system. This is, or rather, was, as described in the narrative. First uncovered in 2017 by the French National Gendarmerie, intelligence and collaboration between the National Gendarmerie, Dutch Police and the National Crime Agency here in Britain resulted in what Jannine van den Berg of the Dutch National Police Force described as 'sitting at the table where criminals were chatting amongst themselves.'

To put the French/Dutch and later our own NCA combined operation in perspective, here are some figures. At the time of its closure, there were in excess of 60,000 subscribers.

The Dutch convictions number in the hundreds. They seized more than eight tonnes of cocaine, around 1.2 tonnes of crystal meth. Nineteen synthetic drug laboratories were smashed, dozens of guns, luxury cars and around 20million in cash. In Rotterdam in 2020, authorities found police uniforms, stolen vehicles, 25 firearms and 25kg of drugs. In a warehouse elsewhere, a 'torture chamber' was unearthed consisting of seven cells made out of sound proofed shipping containers. Inside were Dentist's chairs, hedge trimmers, scalpels and pliers.

Criminal in Ireland were similarly discomfited, police uncovering €1.1m in a flat and €5.5m in cannabis.

In the UK, where 10,000 Encrochat users proliferated, police initially arrested 746 individuals, intercepted two tonnes of drugs with a street value in excess of £100 million, seized £54 million in cash, submachine guns, handguns, grenades and more than 1,800 rounds of ammunition. More than 28 million tablets of the sedative Etizolam were found in Rochester, Kent and in Essex and East Anglia 354kg of cocaine were seized, in the West Midlands a further 233kg was discovered. Police Scotland seized 164kg of cocaine, £200,000 worth of cannabis and £750,000 in cash. In May 2020, police found two suitcases containing £1.1 million in Sheffield. A significant number of murders were thwarted or solved. By 9th October 2023, this operation, codenamed Venetic, had led to more than 3,100 arrests, 1,240 convictions and a combined 7,938 years in prison. The operation recovered 173 firearms, 3459 rounds of ammunition and more than 9 tonnes of Class A drugs.

There's more, but you get the drift.

Acknowledgements

There were rumours regarding the Westland Scout shutting down in mid-flight. These were confirmed and clarified by Dave Wells, Chief Engineer at Historic Helicopters. www.historichelicopters.com Grateful thanks extended to Stuart

Bayliss for initiating the contact. The Triumph Herald switch replacement is artistic licence but at least four Scout helicopters suffered an engine shutdown as a result of poor cockpit ergonomics. The autorotational qualities of the Scout were described as 'startling' by pilots.

On a personal note, we were sorry to have to let Sid go. But it's in the nature of these things that casualties occur, and Themis couldn't keep getting away with it, someone had to die. We hope you feel, as we do, that he went with dignity. Greater love hath no man…

Well, folks, that's it for our third. The fourth in the series is in the planning stage. As you may be aware, we research quite heavily. For purely unselfish reasons then, we need to take a trip to Rome.

Please take the time to go back to where you bought this novel. A simple click and a few words go a long way. In other words, please leave a review. It's important. Can't say why. Goes against the creed.

Thanks G and J.

Printed in Great Britain
by Amazon

37324355R00165